"How d...

"I don't know, Xa... going."

"We don't have to know right away. I've regretted losing you all these years. When I saw you at the diner, I couldn't help myself. I wanted to see if the magic was still there."

"Is it?"

"Oh, yeah."

He craved Rose's touch. The more he had of her, the more he wanted. But if things went wrong they wouldn't have the luxury of walking away from one another again. They had a son to consider.

"Joey's important, but these past weeks haven't just been about our son. They've been about us, too. I want to see where this can go, Rose."

"So do I. But I don't want to be your dirty little secret..."

* * *

Heir to Scandal is a Secrets of Eden story: Keeping their past buried isn't so easy when love is on the line.

* * *

If you're on Twitter,
tell us what you think of Harlequin Desire!
#harlequindesire

Dear Reader,

When I was developing the Secrets of Eden miniseries, it was a joy to get to know each of the brothers. They are all so different and wonderful in their own ways. Wade is the responsible older brother who never felt good enough. Brody is shy, brilliant and terrified he'll never fall in love. Heath is the smarty-pants who uses humor to avoid the serious issues in life. Xander is the smooth one. As a politician, he always knows what to say and do. He repels scandal like a freshly waxed car repels rain.

So of course I had to find a way to put a dent in his armor and find out what is hiding beneath that flawless facade. And who better to do it than the woman from his past who could ruin everything he's worked so hard to build? Rose is the girl who got away: Xander's Achilles' heel. It was so fun to write their story because when Xander falls, he falls hard!

If you enjoy Xander and Rose's story, tell me by visiting my website at www.andrealaurence.com, like my fan page on Facebook or follow me on Twitter. I'd love to hear from you!

Enjoy,

Andrea

HEIR TO SCANDAL

—

ANDREA LAURENCE

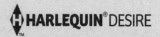

Recycling programs
for this product may
not exist in your area.

ISBN-13: 978-0-373-73339-2

HEIR TO SCANDAL

Printed in U.S.A.

ANDREA LAURENCE

is an award-winning contemporary romance author who has loved books and has been writing stories since she learned to read and write. She always dreamed of seeing her work in print and is thrilled to be able to share her books with the world. A dedicated West Coast girl transplanted into the Deep South, she's working on her own "happily ever after" with her boyfriend and five fur-babies. You can contact Andrea at her website, www.andrealaurence.com.

One

Strawberries. The leading story on the news was about strawberries. No murders, no robberies, no political scandals. "Xander," he said to himself with a wry chuckle, "you're not in D.C. anymore."

Xander Langston had been glued to the local news tonight, as he had been for the past two nights, waiting for things to hit the fan. He'd come home to Cornwall to handle the fallout, but so far the local broadcasts had focused on the unseasonably mild weather, the local youth baseball team's successes and the upcoming strawberry festival. He flipped off the old fuzzy television in the living room and tossed the remote onto the coffee table. He was ordering a flat-screen television for the bunkhouse *and* the main house the next time he got on his laptop. He wouldn't have time to drive into Canton and buy them in person.

If the biggest buzz around town was the Strawberry Days Festival, life was good. No news was good news—

especially with his first book hitting shelves next week and an election year coming up. His critics liked to point out that he'd been elected the first time only because his predecessor and mentor, beloved longtime congressman Walt Kimball, had hand-selected him to follow in his footsteps. Whatever the reason, Xander had succeeded in a landslide victory over his opponent. At the time, he was one of the youngest congressmen ever elected to the U.S. House of Representatives, just making the age requirement of twenty-five.

This fall he would be kicking off yet another reelection campaign and Xander would prefer to remain gainfully employed. That meant a solid voting record, no sound bites that could be taken out of context and absolutely no scandals of any kind. Typically, it was easy for Xander to avoid scandals. He wasn't married, so he couldn't have affairs. He didn't have an interest in prostitutes. He'd never been offered any bribes, and even if he had, he would have turned them down.

But everyone had a skeleton in their closet, so to speak. And that was why he was back in Connecticut at the Garden of Eden Christmas Tree Farm watching this crappy television instead of burning the midnight oil in his Capitol Hill office.

With a sigh, Xander got up from the couch and walked over to the window. The sun had already disappeared behind the rolling green hills, but it was still light enough to illuminate the farm. For as far as the eye could see, there was nothing but balsam and Fraser fir trees.

It was a startling view after being away for so long. Looking out the window of his office in the Longworth House Building earned him an excellent view of the Capitol Building and the sea of tourists and buses traveling up and down Independence Avenue. Those people traveled thousands of miles for the sights he ignored on a daily basis. He was too busy to appreciate the classic architecture and historic significance surrounding him. Most of the time, he took the underground tunnels to the Capitol Building and missed it entirely.

He might have a plush, professionally decorated town house a few blocks from the office in the Capitol Hill district, but this place—with its old, worn furniture and acres of trees—was home. This was where he'd grown up. Being back here, surrounded by the calming influences of nature and fresh air, Xander felt more at ease than he had since he left home for Georgetown and a fast-track career in politics. There was no traffic gridlock here, no honking cabs, no frantic running through the metro stations. He could finally breathe.

Things wouldn't stay peaceful here for long, though. The literal skeleton in Xander's closet belonged to Tommy Wilder and last Christmas it had been unearthed by a construction crew on land that used to be part of the farm. So far there had been no luck in identifying the body, but that would soon change. Brody, his computer-genius foster brother and one of the four "Eden boys," had emailed them all about a week ago with news that the police had commissioned a facial re-creation sketch, but it hadn't been released to the public yet. Xander hadn't asked how Brody knew about it. He was just grateful for the heads-up.

When the sketch hit the news, people would start sniffing around the farm for answers. They'd garnered some attention when the body was first unearthed, but no one really believed it had anything to do with his foster parents, Ken and Molly Eden. The sketch would change that. When Tommy was identified, it would place the dead teenager in their care and people would be forced to consider their involvement. His foster parents weren't fit to deal with the journalists and police that would knock on their door looking for information. Ken was recovering from a heart attack and Molly would be too distraught by the idea of Tommy's death to answer questions. They needed someone at the farm to run interference and Xander was the best choice.

From a very early age, he'd had a way with people. He could talk anyone into anything. His mother used to tell everyone he was a born politician. Ladies found him charming. His constituents described him in a poll as "trustworthy, well-spoken and honest." He would use every tool in his arsenal to fight off the press and protect his family.

Xander had been back in Cornwall for two days and so far nothing but Little League and strawberries. That meant he should really take advantage of the peace to run the errand he'd been considering since he arrived home.

He picked up the hardback book on the coffee table and admired his handiwork. "*Fostering Faith* by Xander Langston," he read aloud. It was still a little surreal even after having author copies for a month already. He'd never intended on writing a book, especially a memoir. Xander had never thought his life was particularly exciting, but the publishing house that had approached him about the project felt otherwise. He was a young and successful congressman whose parents had died tragically and young, thrusting him into the foster-care system. Apparently, that was nonfiction gold.

It had taken a year to write between his official duties and volunteer work at the D.C. Fostering Families Center. Knowing a portion of the proceeds would go to his favorite cause had kept him going when he was stuck in the middle of chapter seven. That and the hefty advance he'd have to return if he changed his mind.

The book came out next week. There would be a charity gala and signing in a couple weeks back in D.C. to raise money for the Fostering Families Center. Hopefully, his reason for coming home wouldn't sink his plans and his sales.

While he was in Cornwall, he wanted to make one special personal delivery. He'd already given copies to his foster parents and his brothers and sister, of course, but he'd brought an extra one on this trip for his high school sweetheart, Rose Pierce. She'd featured heavily in the book as one of the best things to ever happen to him. He wanted her to have an autographed copy and he needed to give it to her in person.

Xander looked down at his watch. It was after seven. His foster brother Wade now lived in Cornwall and had told him that Rose still worked most evenings at Daisy's Diner, just up the highway. This seemed like the perfect time to go. Tonight was Molly's night to play Bunco, so he was on his own for dinner anyway.

He could deliver the book and get a good meal. Daisy's had been a favorite haunt of his teenage years. Rose had worked at the diner back then, too, and he'd wasted many an hour sitting at the counter, sipping milkshakes and talking to her between customers.

Xander climbed into his black Lexus SUV and decided he would get a milkshake tonight for old times' sake, especially if Rose would make it for him. He couldn't remember the last time he'd had one. It might have been the summer before he left for Georgetown. The August heat and his lovesick heart had lured him to the diner nearly every day for a chocolate shake and a few last moments with Rose.

Once he'd left town, life had started moving so quickly. Years had flown by in what felt like minutes. His trips back to Cornwall had been short and infrequent. Lately, he was more interested in a crisp Chardonnay with his meal than a tall glass of chocolate ice cream. Daisy's Diner and its milkshakes had become a distant memory from his childhood.

But not Rose.

He still remembered touching her as if it were yesterday. They had been each other's first loves—that young, passionate, all-consuming and overly dramatic love. You never forgot about that. If it were up to him, he would've taken her with him to D.C. He'd asked, damn near begged, but she wouldn't go. She'd had a terminally ill mother and admission to a nearby college that allowed her to stay close to home and care for her.

He'd understood, but he hadn't liked it. He'd also attempted to meet her demand that he go on to Georgetown and forget about her. He'd avoided her when he came to town. He'd even skipped their high school reunion, but he'd realized that forgetting about Rose was impossible. He'd always remember those big brown eyes and pouty lips. He'd always wonder what happened to her.

No longer. Tonight he was going to focus on tracking her down and catching up on lost time. Writing the memoir had brought his memories of Rose to the forefront of his mind. Now that he was back in Connecticut, he had to see her and he wouldn't be distracted from this task, not even by Tommy Wilder's corpse.

Xander pulled into the gravel parking lot at Daisy's. It was a Thursday night and not a particularly busy one if the cars in the lot were any indication. Through the front windows he could see a couple old guys drinking coffee at the counter and a family in the corner booth. He didn't see Rose, but perhaps she was in the kitchen.

He went inside and opted for a booth near the entrance. It was fairly warm in the diner, making him wish he'd chosen a polo shirt and khakis instead of the long-sleeved dress shirt and blazer he had on. He slipped out of his navy Armani jacket and hung it on the coat hook before he sat down on the red leather bench and tossed the book beside him.

The menus were clipped in a metal stand behind the ketchup and the napkin dispenser, so he reached over and started studying. Not much had changed since he'd been here aside from the prices. They still had milkshakes and his favorite bacon cheeseburger with barbecue sauce and crispy onion rings.

It was a heart attack on a platter, but tonight he wouldn't worry about that. He never got to eat casual, home-cooked food like this in D.C. There it was nothing but expensive multicourse meals at gourmet restaurants. Quick lunches included fresh hand-rolled sushi or gyros and falafel from the carts on the street. But the common feature was always eating while working; talking legislation and deals with other political insiders over a meal was standard practice.

This diner made him feel as if he were seventeen all over again. The only thing missing was—

"Hey there, can I get you something to drink?"

Xander looked up and found himself lost in the wide brown eyes that headlined his teenage fantasies. Rosalyn Pierce, his first love, standing right in front of him after all this time, as though he were dreaming while he sat there.

"Xander?" she said, her jaw initially dropping in surprise before she tightened her lips into a stiff line of concern. She was real. His fantasy Rose would've climbed into his lap and nibbled on his ear as she used to.

"Rose," he replied, his mouth suddenly dry. He'd come here specifically looking for her, yet finally coming face-to-face with her threw his entire body for a loop. "Wade mentioned I could find you at Daisy's. I'm so glad you're still working here...." His voice trailed off when he realized it sounded as if she hadn't done much with her life in the past decade. Rose's guarded expression was proof enough of that. Normally he would've phrased that better, but seeing Rose had robbed him of his usual polished poise. "I apologize—that didn't come out right."

She gave him a watery smile and shook her head. "Not to worry. Most people aren't lucky enough to turn their after-school job into a full-time career like I did. If it helps at all, there was a five-year gap where I didn't even step foot in the building, but they couldn't keep me away forever."

A million thoughts raced through Xander's mind and he fought to put them in some sort of order. His heart began pounding in his chest as if he were in a live televised debate and had just been thrown a curveball question by the moderator. Fortunately, he performed best under pressure.

Rose was as beautiful as he remembered, maybe even more so. In high school she'd been just a girl on the verge of becoming a woman. Now her familiar curves were more lush, making the little cotton uniform cling more deliciously than he recalled. Her long straight brown hair was pulled into a sleek ponytail that fell over her shoulder. The tip teased at the swell of her breasts, allowing his gaze to follow to her cleavage and, eventually, over to her name tag. It still read Rosalyn P., as it had in school.

Had no one snatched her off the market yet? He quickly glanced at her ring finger, which was as bare as his own. That was a crime. A woman like Rose should've been married years ago to a man who appreciated and worshipped her. Sometimes he wished that man had been him. He should've fought for her, asked her to marry him and not taken no for an answer, but how could he ask her to leave her mother when she was so ill?

Xander wanted to talk to her, to see what she'd been

doing since the last time he saw her. She'd left Cornwall to go to Western Connecticut University when he went to Georgetown. The school had a teaching hospital where her mother was being treated and a great elementary education program. She loved kids and had wanted to teach. What had happened? Why was she back to waitressing when she had so much potential?

"I meant I was glad you're still working here because it made you easier to find. Do you have time to chat with me and catch up some?"

She glanced around the restaurant, biting at her lip. He couldn't tell if she thought she *shouldn't* or she just *didn't want to* talk to him. There was a hesitation in her that he didn't quite understand. They'd parted well, hadn't they? She'd broken up with him, so if anyone should be upset, it was him, right?

"Maybe in a little bit after this family finishes up. I'm the only server tonight, but they're almost done. In the meantime, what can I get for you to eat?"

Xander turned away from her confusing expression to let his gaze flick back over the menu and then remembered what he'd chosen. "First I think I'll take some iced tea with lemon. Then I'll have the Texan burger with fries and one of your awesome chocolate milkshakes."

Rose stopped writing on her pad and smiled. He could tell she recognized his order even though it had been eleven years since she'd brought him food to the counter. She looked up at him, her expression softening for the first time. "The usual, huh? Some things never change, do they?"

Xander shook his head and held her gaze. Her beauty hadn't faded. His body's reaction to her was just as immediate, powerful and distracting as it had ever been. Every inch of his body had grown tense when he caught a glimpse of her familiar curves and breathed in her perfume. It made him wonder if the magic they'd make under the summer stars would be just as explosive.

"They sure don't. And I'm glad."

Rose had to literally bite her tongue to keep her nerves from getting the best of her. The pain helped her stay focused, although it made it hard to smile with any sort of warmth. *Whatever.* What was important was that she could not panic. Not here. Not now. This was her first real test and she couldn't flunk within a minute of coming face-to-face with Xander Langston.

Oddly enough, she'd spent a good part of the past five years fantasizing about Xander strolling into the diner just like this. Looking just like this. Smiling at her just like this. Maybe picking her up and carrying her off like the end of *An Officer and a Gentleman.*

And yet, in reality, the moment wasn't all she'd hoped for. She was nervous. Anxious. Worried she would say or do the wrong thing and give her secrets away. And while Xander had the fire of unabashed attraction in his eyes, that was it. His blatant appraisal of her sent a rush of awareness through her body. A warmth rose to her cheeks and other places where a fire had not been stoked in a very long time.

Time had not dulled her reaction to Xander. How could it, when he had gotten only more handsome? Age had made his features sharper and his jaw more pronounced, but he still had the same kind eyes and charming smile. She could very easily let herself get swept up in the moment. Unfortunately, he wasn't going to carry her out of the diner and marry her. He *had* come here looking for her, but she wouldn't read anything into it. He'd missed their high school reunion a few months ago. Perhaps he'd just come to appease his curiosity and see if she still looked good. As always, hot enough to sleep with but easy to forget about.

That meant the dull ache of arousal would go unsoothed. She wasn't about to make the same dumb mistakes twice.

She forced herself to scratch out his order for the cook and spun off in the direction of the kitchen while she still had the strength to walk away from him. It had been hard enough the first time, knowing how much was at stake. Somehow, with nothing more than a dinner order between them, it wasn't any easier.

It had been eleven years since she'd laid eyes on Xander Langston. Eleven years! And yet seeing him like this had lit an unwelcome fire in her libido as though they were back in school again. She'd seen him on the news from time to time, especially during the flood of ads around election season, but it didn't do him justice. That sandy-brown hair, those enchanting hazel eyes, those firm muscles disguised by his expensive and well-tailored clothes—there was no resisting it. She'd never been able to tell Xander no. He had this charm about him. Once he set his sights on what he wanted, he could be very persuasive.

For some reason, Xander had wanted her. Rose hadn't even wanted to date him at first. He was handsome, but they were on different paths. He was the high school senior-class president. He played varsity baseball. He was popular, likable and overflowing with what they called "leadership potential." He had a full ride to Georgetown and a bright future ahead of him. Rose had none of those things, then or now. And yet once he'd decided they should date, there'd been no turning him away.

She pushed the ticket across the stainless-steel countertop to Oscar, the night cook. "I need a Texan with extra barbecue sauce."

Oscar grunted and turned to the grill. Normally, Rose

would take the tea out before she made his milkshake, but she wasn't ready to face him again. Instead she busied herself scooping ice cream into the milkshake machine. It was easier than figuring out what she was going to do.

"It's not a big deal," she said aloud, dumping the thick shake into the tall fountain glass. And it wasn't. He was going to come and go, just as he always did. He hadn't spent more than a handful of days in Cornwall since he'd left. Usually it was for the annual Eden gathering at Christmas when the diner was closed. And then he was back to D.C. and his work at the Capitol Building. Neither his attraction to her nor the secrets she kept from him would change that fact.

She didn't know why he was here in the middle of the summer. Or why he'd come to the diner tonight looking for her. He hadn't sought her out in all this time. She'd left Cornwall for several years but had been back for quite a while. She'd received no calls, no letters, no Facebook friend requests. He'd forgotten all about her, as best she could tell. Hopefully, he would be gone again before he could cause her any grief.

And at the same time...*God,* it was good to see him again. She felt almost like an addict who had been given a small hit of her favorite drug. It wasn't enough to scratch the itch, but just a touch of Xander in her bloodstream would start the cravings again. If she wasn't careful, when he left town, she would go through more painful withdrawal symptoms than ever before.

She topped the milkshake with whipped cream and stopped short of putting the cherry on top. Xander never ate the cherry. He always fed it to her.

Why did she still remember all these insignificant things? She wished she could forget all about Xander—from his smile to his preferences to the way he could make her feel with just the simplest touch. But under the circumstances, it was pretty hard to do. Xander would always be a part of her life, whether he knew it or not.

To avoid the temptation of him dangling the cherry for her to eat, she put it back in the jar. She poured his tea, dropped in the lemon and took both the drinks out to his table. She glanced at her other customers on her way there. The family had left. The two older men were nursing their coffees, but it wasn't time to warm their cups yet. They still had half a piece of pie each.

Rose had no excuses to avoid Xander any longer. As she approached, she noticed he was poring intently over a newspaper someone had left on the counter earlier. He didn't even notice her approach. Apparently, he was more firmly embedded in *her* thoughts than she was in *his*. Sadly, that didn't surprise her at all.

She set his milkshake and tea on the table and he looked up, startled. "Here's your milkshake. It will be about ten more minutes on your food."

"Thank you." He looked down at the milkshake with an amused expression on his face. "No cherry?"

He remembered, too. "I didn't think you liked them."

"I do. I always did. I just knew you liked them more."

It was a small thing, trivial, really, and yet the realization was enough to soften her knees beneath her. Those were the kind of things he did that made her succumb to him. His thoughtfulness and giving nature far surpassed his good looks or bright future. She braced her arm on the back of the booth to steady herself. "Would you like me to bring you one?" she asked.

"No, I'd rather you chat with me for a little bit."

Rose sank into the seat, giving her knees a much-needed break. She tried not to fidget nervously while she sat there, but she couldn't help smoothing out her uniform and picking off stray bits of lint. It was easier than looking him in the eye. "So…" she began. "How've you been?"

Xander shrugged. "Busy. I pretty much haven't stopped running since the day I moved away. School was brutal. Law school was worse." He took a heavy draw of his milkshake and smiled. "This is great. You always made the best chocolate shakes. I ended up working for Congressman Kimball," he continued, "and before I knew it, I was taking his place. But that's all boring stuff. What about you?"

Rose arched an eyebrow at him. "I assure you that whatever you've done in the last few years is far more exciting than what I've been up to."

"What happened to school? I thought you wanted to be a teacher."

"And give up this glamorous life?" Rose laughed. "I finished a semester and had to stop. Life got complicated and I never went back. Mom died that spring and I took that pretty hard. I stayed in Danbury for a couple of years and then moved back home when my dad was having some… *issues*…and helped him run his shop. When my brother, Craig, took over the garage and Daisy's owner offered me my job back with benefits, I couldn't turn it down. So here I am."

"Have you married? I was certain someone would've snatched you up by now."

"Uh, no. Not much happening on the love front, but that's nothing new. You were the only man in this whole town to ever notice I existed. Once you left, I went back to being invisible."

That wasn't entirely true. There was one male in town that noticed her. One that loved and adored her. Unfortunately, he looked at her over the kitchen table every morning with the same hazel eyes that were watching her now.

He was one of several complications to her love life, none of which she had any interest in mentioning to Xander.

"You could never be invisible. The men in this town are just blind if they don't see something great right in front of them."

Xander knew just what to say and just how to say it, but it didn't help. She'd pushed him away to avoid more heartbreak. Going with him to D.C. never would've worked, as much as he'd insisted. He'd had a big life ahead of him that she wasn't a part of and she'd understood that. She'd needed to stay with her mother and forge a new life without Xander. Finding out she was pregnant a week after he left hadn't changed anything. It had just made it harder to cope.

"That's sweet," she said, "but a girl can't believe a word you say. You're one of those slick politicians."

"Not entirely," Xander said with a smile. "I'm also an author." He reached down beside him on the booth and placed a book on the table. "I brought this for you."

Rose reached out and picked up the book. A grinning, handsome Xander stared back at her from the glossy cover. *"Fostering Faith,"* she read aloud. "This is great, Xander. Congratulations."

"It's about my childhood and the path that brought me to Washington. It ties in with my work at the Fostering Families Center. The center provides support, training and social activities for foster parents and children in the system."

She cracked open the book and flipped through a few pages. She stopped when she caught a glimpse of her name in the sea of text. "I'm in it?" she asked. Her heart skipped a beat. What on earth would he have written about her in here?

"Yes. I only used your first name, but I couldn't tell the story of my life without including you. You were such an important part of my high school years."

His hazel gaze focused on her, making her chest tighten. She didn't know what to say and even if she had, she couldn't have spoken when he looked at her like that.

"I autographed it to you," he added. "That's why I came down here. I wanted to give it to you in person."

"Thank you," she managed. "I look forward to—"

"Have dinner with me," he blurted out, his eyes widening as though he'd surprised even himself.

The suddenness of his query caught her off guard, too. "I can't. I have to work."

Xander frowned. "You work every day?"

"No," she admitted. "But I'm not off again until Sunday. I figured you'd be long gone from Cornwall by then."

Xander smiled wide and Rose quickly realized that her alibi wouldn't be good enough. "As luck would have it," he said, "I'm going to be in town for a while. A few weeks at least."

"Oh." Knowing Xander, he would ask her to dinner every day until she relented. She didn't have the strength to fight him off for that long.

"So I can take you out to dinner Sunday night?"

No. No, no, no. Her brain could see the problems a mile away. Eventually, she would slip up and say the wrong thing. She'd mention school or Little League or her dad…. That or she'd lose her mind and think it wouldn't hurt to sleep with him again. Then he would leave and she would be crushed. History could not repeat itself. Her heart couldn't take it.

Rose caught a whiff of his cologne. It was a warm, spicy scent that reminded her of hot summer nights and foggy windows. "Okay," she said before she could stop the words. Her body seemed to have different plans from her brain and at the moment, it had control of her vocal cords.

"Great. Where are you living now? I'll pick you up."

"You can pick me up here," she said a touch too quickly, and then felt the need to explain herself. "I live a couple towns over. There's no sense in you driving all the way out there." That was true enough, although there were more reasons for not wanting Xander at her apartment.

"Fair enough, although it's no imposition."

Rose shook her head and glanced down at her watch. She needed to check on his food, warm up Gary's and Pete's coffees, and get some distance between her and Xander so she could think straight again.

"I'd better go grab your burger," she said sliding out of the booth with the book in her hands. With an awkward parting smile, she disappeared into the kitchen. Safely hidden away, she whacked her forehead against the refrigerator door and groaned.

"Order's up," Oscar said, sliding the plate across the counter. "Don't whack your head so hard you forget which table to take it to."

Oh, there was no way she was going to forget, no matter how many times she hit her head. She also couldn't forget that she was an idiot. She was playing with fire. Somehow the idea both thrilled and horrified her. She glanced down at the book in her hands and the handsome face staring back at her before taking a deep, calming breath. It didn't help. Nothing would.

Rose had a *date* with Xander Langston.

Two

At exactly 7:00 p.m. Sunday, Xander pulled his Lexus back into the gravel parking lot of Daisy's Diner. The restaurant was closed on Sunday nights, but there was one vehicle in the lot—a four-door Honda Civic. A smart choice.

That was one thing he'd always appreciated about Rose. She was practical. She'd always been embarrassed by the fact that she had to leave after school and work while the other girls went to cheerleading and band practice. Xander had thought it was industrious of her. She wasn't frivolous with her time or her money. He'd been proud to date a girl who was hardworking and appreciated what she had.

There had been a time when Xander was spoiled. His father had had a good job; his mother had stayed at home. He and his brother, Heath, hadn't wanted for anything. And then, in the blink of an eye, he'd lost everything. Going to live with the Edens had been like a whole new world. They hadn't had a lot of money, but they'd taught him the value of working hard and having pride in what he accomplished. Each member of their patchwork family had helped run the farm. Come December, he'd do nothing but bag and haul Christmas trees and he'd be happy to do it. It had taught him the skills he needed to fight the good fight on Capitol Hill.

Rose hadn't had it easy, either. Her mother had been diagnosed with stage IV cancer her senior year and her father hadn't made much money as a mechanic. She and her two siblings had both worked because they'd had to. Because of it, she'd appreciated things most people took for granted.

As Xander pulled to a stop, the door of the Civic opened and his heart skipped a beat in his chest. Rose stepped out in a chic little black dress. It was sleeveless with a high, almost mandarin-style collar. It also clung to every curve like black liquid latex had been poured over her body. A bright pink belt encircled her tiny waist and matched the pink heels she wore. Rose had been one of the tallest girls in school at five-ten, and with those heels, she would probably look him right in the eye.

He couldn't wait to find out how well their bodies would align with those shoes. Xander put the SUV into Park and got out. "You look lovely," he said.

Rose smoothed her hand over her hair, which was down tonight, framing her face. She gave him a nervous smile. "Thank you."

Xander walked her around his car and then opened the door for her to step inside. The movement made her respectable hemline inch higher, showing off a flash of her creamy, firm thigh. That was enough to make his palms tingle in anticipation of sliding over them. He hadn't asked Rose to dinner with the end goal of sleeping with her, but he certainly wouldn't complain if that was how it ended up. He needed to have a little fun while he was home. Once that drawing of Tommy was released, the rest of his time would be less than pleasurably spent.

He shut the door and got in on the driver's side. "I have reservations for us at this Italian place in the next town. Molly recommended it."

Xander had danced around who he was taking to dinner—that would've sent Molly into a tizzy—but he had asked about a nice place to eat. His foster mother was on a mission to get all of her children married off. Molly loved Rose and if she thought for a second they might reconcile, he wouldn't hear the end of it until they were married with three kids. Cornwall had some decent dining choices, but he'd been gone so long he wouldn't know what was still open. This place was on the new side, about a year old, but it had gotten rave reviews.

"Sounds great," she said as they pulled out onto the main road.

"Have you been there before?"

Rose chuckled and shook her head. "I don't really eat out much, unless you count Daisy's. I usually work the lunch and dinner shifts because they have the best tips."

Xander knew what it was like to work all the time. He was pretty bad about it. If he did eat out, it was with a colleague or he was attending some kind of political event. He couldn't even remember the last time he'd gone out to dinner with a pretty woman who had no connections to politics. That was sad. He needed to make it a point not to talk about his work at all tonight.

"I know what you mean. My days are pretty long, and unlike most of my fellow congressmen, I don't have family to go home to. That just means I have no reason to leave and I work even longer."

"So you've never married, either? Or did you run one off?"

Xander laughed. "If I had married, I probably would've run her off by now. But no, I'm single. Dating is nearly impossible with my schedule, but the pressure is on. Wade's getting married this fall and get this—my brother *Brody* is engaged, too. Can you believe he's beat me to it?"

"Really? Wow. Good for him."

His brother Brody had been in the same grade as he and Rose. Brody was smart but painfully shy thanks to the scars left behind by his abusive father. He'd come to the Garden of Eden after his dad lost it and dumped battery acid on Brody's face. He was never comfortable in his own skin and until recently was never comfortable around women. His fiancée, Sam, had hunted him down like a lioness stalking a gazelle. Brody hadn't even known what had hit him.

"I know. I guess I'd always consoled myself with the fact that I wouldn't be the last to get married. I figured I had plenty of time. I was wrong."

"Don't look at it that way," she said. "It's better to think that if Brody could find someone, there has to be a woman out there for you. You just haven't found her yet."

Or maybe he had and he'd been a fool and thrown his chance away. That thought had crossed his mind more than one time over the years, but even more so as two of his brothers had gotten engaged. Wade and Tori were getting married in a few months. Brody and Sam were marrying in the spring. Thank goodness his younger brother was not the settling-down type. Heath was always quick to find a flaw in the women he dated. He had some ideal that no woman could ever meet. Xander understood. Every woman that drifted into his life was measured against Rose and came up short.

"You were always good at putting a positive spin on things."

"Spin is your department, Congressman Langston. I just call it like I see it."

Somehow, her using his official title struck him wrong. He wasn't even used to her calling him Xander, so his title felt completely alien. In high school she'd called him Z. No one else had ever called him that before or since. "Please don't ever call me that again. With you in that dress, it makes me feel like a dirty politician out with a young girl."

Rose laughed. "I was just using it for effect. I'll stick with Xander from now on."

He slowed and pulled the car into the restaurant parking lot. "Well, I hope you're hungry. Home-style Italian food is not designed for dieters."

"You know me," she said with a smile. "Salads are for rabbits."

Xander laughed, remembering their dates in high school. Rose had enjoyed eating, whereas some girls he'd dated picked at their food and complained they were fat. That had annoyed him then, and it annoyed him now. Back then it was because he'd worked hard to pay for the food they were wasting. Now he had plenty of money but it annoyed him because he didn't enjoy the company of people who couldn't indulge themselves now and then. Everything in moderation, of course, but he didn't want a woman who would run in horror at the thought of splitting a piece of cheesecake with him.

Once inside the restaurant, he was very pleased with Molly's recommendation. The space was warm and inviting. Nice enough that his tailored gray silk suit and tie weren't out of place, but not so fancy that they couldn't relax and enjoy themselves. The wine bottles on display behind the hostess's station were high quality and not the kind you could buy at the liquor store or order down at the local bar, the Wet Hen.

Their table was intimate, in a dark corner of the restaurant. It was lit by the flicker of ivory candles that gave everything a warm golden glow, including Rose's flawless complexion. He'd always admired her peaches-and-cream skin. She'd never worn makeup in high school and she didn't need it now, although she'd lined her eyes and put a glossy color on her lips.

They quickly ordered and settled in. Their waiter brought their wine and bread with oil and herbs.

Rose pulled a hunk of bread off the loaf and moved it to her plate. "So what brings you back to Cornwall, Xander?"

That was a good question. What *had* brought him back to Cornwall? The truth wouldn't work. He'd given Ken and Molly a lame story about needing to get away from D.C. for a few weeks and prepare for the launch of his book. Molly had eaten it up. Ken had been more suspicious, but he was glad to have him home for a while. That story probably worked just as well as anything.

"Congress is out of session. I was feeling a little burned out, so I decided to come home instead of staying in Washington. With my book coming out and a reelection year on the horizon, I needed it. Come the fall, it will be twelve solid months of campaigning and fund-raising on top of finishing out my term. It's exhausting. I needed to get away for a while and recharge before I jump back into the fray."

"That's understandable. When you work that hard for that long, you've got to get away every now and then or you'll go crazy."

Xander couldn't hide his smirk. "Pot, I'd like you to meet kettle."

She shrugged away his dig. "I never said I wasn't crazy.

You just haven't asked me the right questions to uncover the ugly truth."

Xander took a sip of his wine and regarded her across the table. She didn't look a decade older, but there were subtle changes. He could detect the faint lines of stress that life was etching onto her face, but he didn't mind it. He preferred women with faces that actually moved. It was hard to come by anymore. But Rose was real. Fresh and honest and everything he remembered her to be. He'd thought for a while that he'd embellished her in his mind over the years, but she met his every expectation. He hadn't been this entranced by a woman in a very long time.

"You wouldn't be the first crazy woman I found to be incredibly sexy."

Rose probably thought her blush would be disguised by the dim lighting, but he could still make out the pink tint of her cheeks. He wanted to reach across the table and stroke the pad of his thumb across her soft skin, but if he started touching her, he wasn't certain he would be able to stop.

Later tonight perhaps he wouldn't have to. He wanted Rose. He shouldn't. She deserved someone who could offer her more than just a few weeks. But he couldn't change how he responded to her. It was hardwired in his DNA somehow. What would it hurt for them to indulge? It would certainly make his time here more pleasurable.

All of this assuming, of course, that the reason he was home didn't ruin it all.

Xander and his foster brothers hadn't seen the sketch of the unidentified man buried on their property, but the odds were it would lead the authorities back to the farm. Anyone who knew Tommy Wilder back in the day would probably recognize him from the drawing.

What would happen then? Xander, with his law degree, was pretty certain that none of the Eden kids would be charged or serve jail time. Tommy's death was justifiable and the statute of limitations had run out on any stupid things they'd done after the fact. But they were more concerned with the truth coming out. It could kill their father. Break their mother's heart. Ruin his career and the work he did with his charity.

And as far as Rose was concerned, he didn't think she would be so keen on seeing him if he was implicated in the death of one of his fellow foster children. Really, calling Tommy a child was a misnomer. Nearly eighteen, he had been a large, dangerous, out-of-control teenager with sticky fingers and hard fists. The other children had only done what they had to do to protect each other and the home they loved.

Perhaps she would understand. Either way, he would figure it out. If the alternative was staying far, far away from Rose, he would just have to make sure that the Garden of Eden Christmas Tree Farm, and everyone who'd ever lived on it, came out of this squeaky-clean. That was why he was here anyway.

Making love to Rose would just be an exceptionally sweet bonus.

Dinner went by quickly. The wine had flowed, and so had the conversation. She'd tried to keep the conversation focused on his life now or on reminiscing about their childhoods together. Talking about her life was dangerous territory and she wanted to avoid it. It had gone well so far. Before she knew it, their creamy slab of tiramisu was gone and the check had arrived.

As they walked out to the parking lot together, she was surprised to find Xander's black Lexus was the last car out there. The restaurant was so well designed for romance and privacy that you couldn't tell if there were a hundred or a dozen people inside. Apparently, there were none. "I didn't realize we closed the place down."

Xander walked her around to the passenger side of the SUV but stopped short of opening the door. "I'm not ready for tonight to be over yet."

Neither was she. She'd been hesitant to spend this time with Xander, but she'd had a nice evening. This was the first real date she'd gone on in forever. Adult time with nice clothes and good food and, for once, no worries. She had thoroughly enjoyed herself and she didn't want to go home and start her old life back up again. "It doesn't have to be," she said.

The skies were dark and clear tonight. The nearly full moon hung overhead, casting everything in a silvery light. It made it hard to read Xander's expression, but his tense body language made it clear he was holding something in. She wanted to put her hand to his cheek and urge him to tell her what he wanted to say.

"Rose…" he said, hesitating for a moment. "I've waited eleven long years to kiss you again. When I was writing the chapters about our time together, I realized how special you were to me. And the moment I saw you in the diner, kissing you again was all I could think about. I've missed the feel of your lips and the soft sounds you made when I touched you just right."

Rose's breath caught in her throat. Had he really been thinking of kissing her all this time? She didn't know what to say. It was the most romantic thing she'd heard in a long time. Maybe ever. Every joint in her body softened like room-temperature butter as he spoke the words to her.

He ran his hand through his hair and shook his head softly. "I know I have no right to ask anything of you, because I'm not staying around for long, but I'd kick myself if I let you out of my sight and didn't at least…" His voice trailed off. Then his gaze zeroed in on her own. "May I kiss you?"

She knew she should say no for a million reasons, but none of them mattered at the moment. Not with the intense way he was looking at her. His eyes were devouring her as if she were a cool glass of water and he were stranded in the desert. It felt nice to be that desired again. How could she turn that down? Besides, what could a kiss hurt? Just one harmless little kiss? It didn't mean anything. As long as she kept the situation in perspective, it would be fine.

"How could a girl say no to that?"

Xander smiled and his elusive dimples appeared. Suddenly, she was seventeen again and his boyish charm melted away all her defenses. He stepped forward until her back was pressed against his SUV. He reached out to touch her face, cradling her cheek against his palm. Rose couldn't keep from closing her eyes and leaning into his touch.

"You are so beautiful," he whispered, his lips centimeters from her own.

She could feel the featherlight caress of his breath as he spoke. A chill ran down her spine, making her shiver softly. He brought his palms to her upper arms, gently rubbing up and down to warm her skin. His hands were large and masculine. Not rough, but powerful as they held her. He closed his eyes for a moment. Rose wondered if he was reconsidering kissing her. She couldn't bear the thought.

"Xander?" she said, barely louder than a breath.

His eyes opened and then…contact. Xander's mouth pressed softly against hers. The moment their lips touched, it was as though they'd never been apart. The suppressed passion reignited and the chaste first-date kiss quickly unraveled into the heated embrace of old lovers.

His tongue sought hers out, gliding like silk into her

mouth. She drank him in, losing herself in the pleasurable buzz of the wine and the hum of desire moving through her nervous system.

It had been so long since she'd let herself indulge with a man. Any man, much less Xander. He was the one who knew her every hope and dream. The one she'd given her virginity to. Her heart to. And through some weird twist of fate, here she was, back in his arms again.

Xander broke away from their kiss, but only to move on to new, unexplored parts of her body. His hungry mouth traveled over the curve of her throat, tasting her skin and nipping gently with his teeth. Rose clutched at him, tilting her head back to give him better access. Her neck was always so sensitive and he remembered it. Every caress sent a shiver of pleasure down her spine that urged her to press against the hard wall of his body.

Xander moved his hands over the soft fabric of her dress. She could feel the heat of his skin penetrating her clothes and warming her body. His touch was electric, bringing to life each neglected part of her body as he caressed it. Her breasts tightened and ached painfully against the confines of her bra. Her stomach tensed and twitched under his fingertips, her center nearly boiling over with the need he quickly built in her.

Her blood raged through her veins as her heart pounded faster and faster. There was no denying that she wanted Xander. The moment he asked her to dinner, she'd known this was an eventuality. She couldn't tell him no and right now she didn't want to. She'd missed him. Missed his touch. And even if he would be disappearing back to D.C. in a short time, she would have these memories to keep her satiated.

Rose gasped as his hand cupped her breast and squeezed gently. She arched her body into his, pressing her stomach against the hard ridge of his desire. She drew her leg up, hooking it around his thigh. His hand moved to her exposed skin, gliding along the slit of her dress. They were in the middle of a parking lot, but she didn't care. He groaned against her throat, whispering her name into her ear.

It was the most erotic thing she'd ever heard. Giving herself to Xander might not be the right choice, but in that moment, she didn't care. She wanted him.

And then her cell phone rang.

It was her brother's ringtone. The passionate haze she'd lost herself in quickly evaporated. Considering he knew she was on a date, there had to be something wrong. And if there wasn't, she was going to whip him good with her shoe the minute she got home.

"I'm sorry," she said, pushing gently at the lapels of Xander's suit and reaching for her purse. "It's my brother, Craig. I've got to take this."

Xander nodded and took a step back to give her breathing room and some privacy. She pulled out the phone and answered, her voice still shaky with desire. "Yes?" she said, her tone pointed despite its breathy quality.

"I know," Craig said. "And I'm sorry. But I had to call. Joey fell off my trampoline in the backyard. I'm pretty sure he's broken his left arm. I'm on my way to the E.R. right now. I figured you would want to meet me there."

Rose could hear Joey's whimpers in the background. Her poor baby. He'd never broken any bones before, which was surprising considering how active he was. She'd told Craig about fifteen times that she didn't like those big trampolines. They were just made for breaking children. And now she'd proved her point. Her son was looking at a cast for weeks and it would probably mean that he'd miss out on the Little League championship later this month. They had a five-round bracket to play through, then on to the regional play-offs in early August. They had the best team the area had seen in a long time and really had a shot at going all the way. Joey would be devastated.

And all so she could go on a stupid date she never should've said yes to in the first place. It was a horrible interruption, but now she was thankful for it. The call had given her a moment to gather herself and realize she was about to make a huge mistake with Xander. This was the man who'd left Cornwall and forgotten she'd ever existed. Eleven years and one charming smile later and she was on the verge of sleeping with him. What was wrong with her? Had she no self-respect?

"Yes, go. I'll meet you there as soon as I can. Tell him I'm on my way." Rose turned off her phone. "I've got to go."

Xander nodded, his fists shoved deep into his pockets. "I gathered that much. Is everything okay?"

"No. I have to go to the hospital to meet Craig." Her hands were shaking as she attempted to slip her phone into her purse and ended up dropping it onto the pavement.

Xander dipped down to pick it up and hand it to her. "Let me drive you. It's a long trip to the nearest hospital and you're too shaken up to drive yourself."

"I'm fine, really. I just need you to take me back to my car."

"No. You're upset. I don't want you getting in a wreck." His eyes were dark in the dim light of the parking lot, but their plea was unmistakable.

Then she remembered. His parents had died in a head-on collision when a teenage girl had swerved into their lane. She had survived and told the cops she'd been crying at the wheel because her boyfriend had dumped her. Of course he'd be concerned that she was too emotionally compromised to drive. "Okay. Thank you," she said without thinking through what she would do when they got to the hospital.

Xander helped her into the SUV and they immediately pulled out onto the highway. They were several miles down the road before either of them spoke again.

"May I ask what happened? Is there anything I can do?"

Rose clutched her purse tightly against her and softly shook her head. "Thank you, but there's not much to be done unless you're an orthopedist. It seems he broke his arm on the trampoline."

"Who? Craig?"

Rose took a deep breath. She could feel the threads of her deception start to unravel. Perhaps she could take a page from the politician's handbook and lie by omission. Tell what she had to but not all of it.

"No," she said. "My son."

Three

There was a long, uncomfortable silence after Rose spoke. She kept waiting for Xander to say something, but he didn't. The car just kept steady and even, heading for the hospital. She supposed that she should say something, but she didn't want to lie to Xander. She'd only ever wanted to protect him from himself. He would've done the right thing, which would've been the wrong thing for him.

"His name is Joey. He's part of the reason I ended up dropping out of college."

She waited for him to push. To ask the big question, but he didn't. When she turned to look at him, his eyes were laser-focused on the road.

"Is he okay?"

Rose let the air she'd been holding out of her lungs. "My brother says he broke his arm. I won't know for sure until after he sees the doctor. Hopefully, it won't require surgery. As it is, he's going to end up missing the Little League regional championship. He's going to be crushed."

"I saw on the news that one of the local teams was doing well."

"Yes. They won for our county, which made them eligible to play in the regional tournament in a few weeks. It probably won't be long enough for him to play. I feel so bad for him. He loves baseball."

"I played in Little League for several years, although we never came close to winning any tournaments. The summers of my childhood were always filled with night games and popcorn from the concession stands. I quit the league when my parents died. Playing in high school was never quite the same."

"I liked watching you play. And I like watching Joey play, too, when I can go. A lot of times, Craig has to take him because I'm working."

"That must be hard, missing out on things."

Rose shrugged away his concerns. Lots of things in life were hard, but you did what you had to do. "Someone has to pay for Little League. It's not cheap. Neither is clothing a boy that seems like he grows an inch a month. He's not even a teenager yet."

"You won't be able to keep enough food in the house," Xander said teasingly. "I remember when all the boys hit their midteen growth spurts. Molly was having fits trying to keep us fed. It was impossible."

"Craig was like that. I think that was half the reason he ended up getting a job at a fast-food place. He ate most of his salary."

Rose could see the lights of the hospital in the distance. Xander slowed down and pulled into the parking lot near the emergency-room entrance. He found a spot and turned off the engine. She was anxious to get inside to Joey, but she could sense a hesitation in Xander. She waited a moment and at last he spoke.

"Rose, why didn't you mention that you had a son before? We've been talking for hours. I would think that would come up in the conversation."

Panic seized her, tightening her chest like a vise clamped on to her lungs. Her mind raced for an answer. "Honestly, tonight was about being back in high school again." These words were true, if not entirely so. "You were attracted to me, just like the old days. I didn't want to ruin the fantasy of our reunion by mentioning I was a single mother."

"Why would that ruin it?"

Rose shrugged. "Because then I'm not the sexy girl from high school. I'm the single mother you used to date, complete with her own set of baggage."

"Everyone has baggage."

Boy, didn't she know it. Joey wasn't even the half of it. "I'm sorry not to bring him up. I'd better get inside. Thank you for driving me."

Rose reached for the handle of the door but realized as she climbed out that Xander was getting out, too. Was he coming in with her? Why would he do that? Damn it. He was too thoughtful.

She rounded the hood of the car and stepped into his path. "You don't need to go in with me."

"I know that." He ignored her protests and took her elbow, guiding her toward the building. "You're upset. I'm going to walk you inside."

With every step closer to the door, Rose could feel the noose tightening around her neck. There was no way that Xander would be able to look at her son and not realize the truth. Until he was about four, Joey had been a towhead and looked more like her sister than anyone. That and distance from Cornwall had bought her time from questions. But now Joey was so much the image of his father that sometimes it was painful for Rose to look at him. They had the same light brown hair, the same wide golden-hazel eyes. Joey had her nose and lighter complexion, but everything else was his father, especially as he got older. In a few years, he'd develop the same strong build and square jaw.

If Xander went into the patient area with her, there'd be no hiding it. Or denying it. As they pushed past the information desk into the E.R. waiting room, she wondered if she should stop and tell him the truth. Put an end to the hiding and the worries. At the very least, warn him before they got inside. They were in the middle of a crowded emergency room, surrounded by strangers with a variety of injuries and infectious diseases. It wasn't the ideal place or time, but when exactly was? She couldn't go back eleven years and change things. She either had to tell him or send him home. At least here there were too many witnesses for him to kill her.

"Xander?" She hesitated outside the door that would lead to the pediatric triage area. "Before I go in there, I need to tell you something."

"Right now?" His brow knit together in concern. "Don't we need to get back there to Joey?"

"I do," she said. This was the moment. She could confess. The words were on the tip of her tongue. Then she chickened out. "But you don't. Please go home. It's late."

Xander frowned, his hazel eyes searching her face for answers. "Why do you—?"

"Rose!" The triage door opened and Craig came out.

"We're coming," Xander replied.

The expression on Craig's face was unmistakable. Her brother was not Xander's biggest fan. He'd been around all these years, acting as Joey's surrogate father. He probably blamed Xander for not being there, although it wasn't his fault. Rose hadn't told Xander about the pregnancy, because he deserved a better life. He would've walked away from his scholarship to stay in Cornwall and marry her. He would've given up his dreams of a life in politics to work some low-pay unskilled job and support his family.

She wouldn't ask that of him. And she certainly didn't want to ask him to take her back just for the sake of their child after she'd pushed him away. But maybe now that he was a success and Joey was older, the time had come. Fate seemed to be nudging her in that direction.

None of that mattered to Craig. As far as he was concerned, Xander was guilty of having sex with his little sister and that was crime enough. "We?"

"Of course," Xander said. "I'm not just going to drop her on the curb and call our date done because her son is hurt."

"*Her* son," Craig repeated with a smirk. His gaze met Rose's and she felt the urge to shrivel up into herself and disappear. Craig had figured out that Xander didn't know the truth yet. Fireworks were about to fly in the E.R. and he would have a front-row seat. He shouldn't look so damn smug about it, though.

"Shush, Craig. Come on." Resolved to her fate, she took Xander's hand and pulled him behind her. "Where's Joey?"

Craig pointed down the hallway. "He's in the fourth bed down on the pediatric side." He started down the corridor and they both followed.

"Mom!"

The minute her broken child came into view, everything else that was going on no longer mattered. She let go of Xander and rushed over to her son's bedside. They had his left arm in a sling to keep him from moving it.

She hugged him gently and brushed his damp hair back

to press a kiss on his forehead. His skin was pale and moist from coping with the pain. "Hi, baby. How are you?"

"I'm doing a little better," he said with a weak smile. "They gave me some medicine and it doesn't hurt anymore. I also can't feel my lips."

Rose smiled. "That's good. Did they take X-rays yet?"

"No," Craig interrupted. "They're coming to do that in a minute."

Rose nodded but refused to turn and look at Xander. Not yet. She wanted to focus entirely on making sure her son was okay. That was the most important thing.

"Hey, everyone," one of the nurses said, parting the curtains around his bed. She pushed a wheelchair over to where Rose was standing. "I'm going to take Big Shot here over to X-ray to get a look at this arm."

Rose and the nurse helped Joey out of bed and got him settled into the chair. "Do I need to go with him?" She desperately hoped the answer would be yes.

"No, it's better for you all to stay out here. We'll be back in about fifteen or twenty minutes. Take a break. Get a drink. It will be a long night."

Rose watched the nurse roll Joey away. The minute the chair rounded the corner, she heard Xander's quiet, even voice from the other side of the hospital bed.

"I think we need to have a talk, Rose."

She took a deep breath. The moment had come. She had been waiting eleven long years to finally unburden herself of this secret. Unfortunately, it was the kind of secret that was harder to tell the longer you waited. Now she didn't have a choice. Rose nodded softly and shot a glance at her brother that said in no uncertain terms that he was to get out.

Craig gave her a disappointed look and started backing away. "I'm going to go see what they have in the gift shop. Text me if you need me." He disappeared down the hallway.

Now it was just the two of them. And the truth.

"Rose…" His voice trailed off in near disbelief. His palm rubbed over his face, then back over his hair. His hazel gaze was near penetrating as he focused it on her. "Do you have something you need to tell me?"

"I think you already know, Xander. Yes, Joey is your son."

The room felt as if it were spinning around him. Xander reached out and steadied himself on the footboard of the hospital bed. He tried to take a deep breath, but his chest was too tight to draw in the air.

He had a son. A ten-year-old son. And she'd never told him.

Rose sat down on the edge of the hospital bed. "I found out that I was pregnant about a week after you left for college. I was about to leave myself and I wasn't sure what to do. I had broken up with you. You were leaving to do great things…. I decided to just start school and figure it out later. I had time."

"You had a few months, not a few years, Rose." He couldn't keep the bitterness of betrayal from his voice.

"I know. I spent a lot of time at the hospital talking to my mother about my situation. It kept her mind off the treatments and how poorly she felt. She walked me through all my options, but I knew that I wanted to keep our baby. It might be all of you I ever had. She urged me to contact you. You know how moms are. She didn't have much time left and worried about me doing this on my own. She thought you would marry me if you knew."

"I would have."

Rose turned and looked him straight in the eye. "I know. That's why I didn't tell you."

Xander had a hard time processing what she was saying. "You didn't want to marry me?"

"Of course I wanted to marry you. I wanted to go to D.C. with you, but it just wasn't meant to be. I didn't want you to marry me just because of the baby. That wasn't the path you were on, Xander. Look at all you've done in the last eleven years! All that you've accomplished… None of that would've happened if you had come home and married me."

Xander opened his mouth to argue with her, but he was struck with the truth of her words. She was right. Even if she had moved to D.C. with him and they'd gotten an apartment in family housing, finishing school would've been challenging. He'd had a full-ride scholarship with books, room and board, but it wouldn't have covered baby food and clothes and diapers. He would've had to work. It was hard enough to finish school without the distraction of a young family at home.

"It wasn't your decision to make," he said instead.

"I couldn't let you give up everything you worked so hard for because we made one little mistake."

"Little? He's ten years old."

"I know that I should've told you later, maybe, when he was older and you'd finished school. But the longer you keep a secret, the harder it is to tell. I didn't even know where to start."

"So you just waited until you had no choice? No wonder you didn't want to go to dinner and didn't mention *your* son all night. Even when you had the chance, you didn't want to tell me. You've had all these years to do it, but no, you wait for the worst possible time. I'm about to start my reelection campaign. My book comes out in two days. I don't need any scandals right now."

He watched Rose's expression crumble into tears and his chest ached for her, even though he didn't want it to. She had lied to him. Hidden his child from him. And yet she had done it *for* him. She'd sacrificed her own dreams, her own life, to raise Joey on her own and allow him to live his dream.

He wanted to be angry with her. To shake her and let out some of his pent-up aggression, but he just couldn't do it. Instead he sank down onto the foot of the bed. "Please stop crying," he asked.

"I'm sorry," she said. "Everything I've done was to protect your dream. It never occurred to me that Joey and I would still be a liability to your success this far down the road."

"Well, we're lucky, I think. The reporters got bored with me very early on and spend most their time digging up other people's scandals. But the spotlights will be on me during the book tour and the reelection."

"Can we keep it a secret for a while? No one else needs to know yet, right?"

"Perhaps. If we can keep this quiet for a little while, I might be able to defuse the damage. Compared to the things my colleagues have gotten into, this is hardly headline news."

"Okay," she said, her voice quiet.

"Who knows that I'm his father?" Hopefully, the information hadn't spread too far. The fewer people who knew, the easier it would be to contain it. Given that Molly didn't know, it had to be pretty hush-hush.

"For certain? Just the two of us, since Mom passed a few weeks after he was born. My brother knows, but I've never told him directly. He's just pieced it all together over the years."

"How did you explain it to everyone else?"

"I went away to college. I came back a couple years later with a little boy. When people asked, I told them a story about an ill-fated fling at school with a jerk that didn't love me. Everyone seemed to take it at face value. At the time, there were bigger stories than the father of my child."

Xander frowned. What did she mean by that? "Bigger stories about you?"

"Not directly. It was several years ago and not important."

Xander doubted that, but it seemed he could only pull one secret from her at a time. "I'm surprised no one ever asked if he was mine."

"People around here don't see Joey very much. He goes to school in Torrington and I only bring him into Cornwall when I don't have anyone to watch him and I have to work. If people suspect, they've been polite enough to keep it to themselves for the most part. A notable exception was Christie Clark, that catty girl from school. She went to Western Connecticut State, too, and saw me pregnant in the grocery store one day. She asked if you were the father and when I told her no, she told me I was a fool for letting the wrong guy knock me up. I wanted to punch her in the face and I was hormonal enough to almost do it."

Xander felt awful. He knew Rose didn't have it easy in this town as it was. Her family had never had much money and she'd never fit in the popular set. This probably made it that much harder for her.

"I'm sorry you felt like you had to go through all of this alone."

Rose smiled and waved her hand dismissively. "I wouldn't trade Joey for the whole world. Things may not have always been easy, but if I went back in time, I'd make the same decisions. Well, except maybe I would've punched Christie Clark."

At that, Xander had to chuckle. Christie had been a real bitch in school. She thought she was better than everyone else and would always complain loudly that she never understood why Xander had chosen Rose when he could've had her instead. He would've sooner stuck his penis in a box fan.

"So now what?"

Xander looked up at her. She was right. Joey would be back in a few minutes and they had a lot to work out. They could rehash the past and the hows and the whys for hours, but they needed a plan going forward. "I think you're right. I say we agree to keep this quiet for the time being. Especially where Joey is concerned. He's got enough to deal with right now without all that piled on top."

"Agreed," she said, looking a touch relieved. She didn't look as if she were ready to deal with the fallout of her secret, either. "We won't tell anyone until we determine the timing is right for us both."

"I want to acknowledge Joey as my son, and I will, but don't think I can go forward with any legal claims right away. The minute I file the paperwork, some nosy reporter will jump on it, especially if my face is all over the news doing interviews and talking about my charity. But I don't want you to think that means I'm going to shirk off my responsibilities. I do want to help."

"Help?"

"Yes, help. It will be hard with me out of state, but I can send money, at least. I'm sure you could use the extra money for things like school expenses or summer camp. Emergency-room co-pays, perhaps?"

Rose clenched a tight fist of sheets. She was a proud

woman, and he appreciated that about her. He could tell how hard this was for her to accept, but she wasn't a fool. They both knew she could use the help. "I thought public servants weren't paid that well."

"I'm comfortable. The advance of my book was very nice and I made some good money investing. I can absolutely help."

Xander had invested what little money he had in the start-up of Brody's software company. That alone had him sitting pretty, financially. If and when Brody's company went public, the stock would skyrocket. He couldn't tell Rose that detail, however, because people still hadn't connected his brother Brody Butler to mysterious software tycoon Brody Eden.

She nodded at last, giving in. "Thank you. I wasn't sure where I was going to come up with the money for this."

"What about living expenses? You said you had a place pretty far out of town. That has to cost you a lot in gas."

Rose frowned at him. "There's no apartment complexes around here. The closest thing I could get was a two-bedroom apartment over near Torrington."

Torrington was about fifteen miles away. It wasn't a terrible drive, just a straight shot down Highway Four, but it wasn't close, either. In bad weather it could be a nightmare to drive back and forth. "Maybe we can get you a house someplace closer to town."

"A house?" Rose chuckled. "Have you seen the home prices around here?"

"I said I wanted to help, Rose."

"That doesn't mean we have to become a major drain on your finances. Help is help. What you're suggesting is more than that."

"What? More like child support? That's the point.

You've done this on your own for ten years. I have a lot to make up for."

Rose sighed and folded her hands in her lap. "I just don't want to be—"

"We're ba-ack!" the nurse announced, rolling Joey back to his bed.

They both leaped up and hovered anxiously as the nurse helped Joey back onto the hospital bed. "How did everything go?" Xander asked.

"Fine. The doctor should be in to talk to you guys in just a minute. Then, after that, I'm pretty sure the casting crew will be here." The nurse turned to Joey. "Start thinking about what color wrap you want. We have bright blue, neon green, red, hot pink—" she wrinkled her nose and shook her head "—and construction-cone-orange."

"So it's broken?" Rose asked.

"I'm not a doctor, so I'm not supposed to say, but between you and me…*oh, yeah*."

The nurse disappeared with the wheelchair, leaving Rose, Joey and Xander alone together for the first time. He didn't really think about that until he heard Joey ask Rose a question.

"Mom?" he whispered in an attempt to be sneaky, but it was loud enough to hear down the hallway. "Who is that man? Was he your date?"

"Oh," Rose said, putting on her best smile. "I'm sorry, baby. I was too worried about your arm. Joey, this is Mr. Langston. And yes, he was my date. We went to high school together a long time ago."

Xander frowned at the super-formal use of his name for the second time tonight. It was bad enough for Rose to do it. He didn't want his son calling him that, too. "You can just call me Xander."

"Xander?" Joey said, his eyes wide. "I wouldn't even know how to spell that."

"No worries," he said. "There won't be a test."

"Good," Joey said with a wide smile that was so much like his own at that age. There was even a hint of his same dimple in his left cheek.

The first moment he'd laid eyes on Joey, he'd known the truth. There were pieces of both him and Heath at that age in the boy. His brother had better well not be the father of his ex-girlfriend's baby, so that left only one answer.

It had actually thrown him for a loop seeing Joey lying in that hospital bed. Xander hadn't been with his parents the night of their car accident. He had been spending the night at a friend's house after going to see the latest superhero movie. Heath had been with them, though.

The next morning, his friend's parents had brought him to the hospital, not quite sure what to do with the child who'd become an orphan while they'd watched him overnight. His father had been killed immediately and his mother had been on life support in a coma she wouldn't wake up from. Heath had been in stable condition, but he had been hurt pretty badly—a broken leg, a laceration across his forehead and a few cracked ribs.

When he'd gone into the hospital room and seen Joey for the first time, he'd looked just like Heath had. He'd almost had a flashback to the most traumatic moment of his life in that instant. And then to realize that it wasn't his brother lying there but his *son*...

"How are we feeling, Joey?" The doctor stepped in, X-rays gripped tightly in his hands.

"I think the medicine is starting to wear off," Joey said, favoring his arm.

"We'll get you some more. But first let's talk about what you managed to do to yourself."

The doctor flipped on the light panel and threw one of the X-rays up onto it. Xander wasn't a medical professional, but even he could see the slight displacement of one bone and the crack in the other bone of his forearm.

"You've given your radius a good whack. Cracked your ulna, too. The good news is you won't need surgery. This should come back together just fine with a cast. And since you're right-handed, this shouldn't interfere as badly with daily activities. You'll have a cast for a few weeks, and then we can switch you into a brace. The bad news is, I'm afraid this baseball season may be over before you can play again."

Joey's face tightened as he tried not to show how upset he was. He was determined to be a man and not cry, but clearly he wanted to. Xander understood. Baseball had been his life at that age. Losing it when his parents died had been just one more tragedy piled on the rest. At least his son would get to play next season.

"I'll bet they'll save me a good seat to watch from the dugout," Joey offered cheerfully, his lower lip barely quivering as he held in his disappointment.

He was ever the optimist, just like his mother.

"The crew will be in here to get you all plastered up. Did you decide what color you want your cast to be?"

"Green," Joey said. "That's my favorite color."

Xander met Rose's gaze across the hospital bed and she smiled softly. She had probably been noticing the similarities between her son and her lover for years, but it was all new to him and somehow surreal. Green was Joey's favorite color.

It was his, too.

Four

It was nearly three in the morning when Xander turned off the main highway toward her apartment complex. They'd opted to leave her car at the diner. Craig would take her to work the next day and she could get it then.

They didn't talk much on the drive home and Rose was relieved. She was emotionally and physically exhausted. Tonight had been a night eleven years in the making and now it was done. All she wanted to do was get her baby into bed, make him comfortable, give him some pain medication and pass out herself.

Rose glanced over her shoulder at the slumped-over bundle in the backseat. Joey was out cold, as was to be expected. Between the late hour and the medication, he didn't stand a chance. She was just happy that he could sleep, considering the heavy, uncomfortable cast on his arm. He actually looked quite peaceful. Rose had always enjoyed watching him sleep. The first night she brought him home from the hospital, she'd just sat in her rocking chair and watched him in his bassinet.

Then and now he was like an angel in a painting with peach skin and dark eyelashes against his rose-kissed cheeks. His lips were full and pouty, like hers, and they moved ever so slightly as he dreamed. He was getting older, and his cherubic face was fading into the lean features of his father, but she couldn't help but look at him and see her baby again.

"He's been out since we pulled onto the highway," Xander said. "Poor guy."

Rose smiled at her son and turned back to face the road. "He's had a long day. I hate to wake him up to get him inside, but he's gotten too big to carry anymore."

"We'll figure it out," Xander said. "We might be able to walk him in without fully waking him up. I used to sleepwalk. All you had to do was stand me up and guide the way. By the way…does your brother live near you?"

"No," Rose said. "He has a house in Litchfield."

"Well, then is there any particular reason why your brother is following us to your place? It's a little late to preserve your honor."

"What?" Rose turned again, this time to look at the truck following behind them. It was Craig, all right. His truck was jacked up on big wheels and one headlight was fading out. "That's odd. He didn't mention coming back with us. He should've turned off onto 63 a couple miles back."

Xander made a thoughtful humming sound but didn't respond. Instead he listened intently as Rose gave him the last bit of instructions to lead him to her building. He pulled into a vacant spot and her brother's truck rolled into the one beside them.

Rose and Xander climbed out of his SUV, meeting Craig as he opened the back door of the Lexus. "You didn't have to come all the way back with us. I know it's late and you have to work tomorrow."

"It's no problem," Craig said, giving Xander an appraising look before he reached in and scooped up Joey into his arms. Even in his sleep, Joey clung to him like a monkey and Craig brushed past them toward the apartment.

Rose noticed the slightly annoyed expression on Xander's face. He'd been a dad officially for only a few hours now, but he seemed perturbed to lose his opportunity to fill the role. At the same time, her brother wasn't about to step aside. He'd been Joey's father figure since the day he was born.

She expected Xander to say something about it, but he shook it off and shut the door.

"It's late for you, too," she said, looking up at the handsome man who'd anticipated only a nice date with an old friend tonight. This was not at all how she'd planned this night to end, either. Things had taken a sharp left turn the moment her brother called. Part of her wished she could wind back the clock and change the way the night ended, but another part of her was relieved to have all the secrets out in the open. Well, at least the ones relevant to Xander.

He smiled and reached out to take her hand. "I don't have to work tomorrow."

She felt so tiny and delicate wrapped in the massive warmth of his fingers. It felt like electric sparks were dancing up her arm when their skin touched, making her tremble softly. When he lifted her knuckles to his lips, her breath moved almost as rapidly into her lungs as her heart beat in her chest. She responded even to the most simple and innocent of Xander's gestures. She wished she didn't. It would be easier to tell him no. That was the right thing to do. Son or no son, he would be going back to D.C. soon. If she wasn't careful, he would leave heartbreak in his wake.

He still had her hand clasped in his when he spoke again. "Besides, I'm twelve feet from your apartment. It would be stupid not to see this date through to the very end. May I walk you to your door, Rose?"

"You may." It was safe with Craig still there. Even if she wanted to, she couldn't invite Xander in. She took his arm and walked with him down the narrow sidewalk that led to her apartment door. It was already open and judging by the light in the hallway, Craig was inside getting Joey into bed.

"I'm sorry about his arm," Xander said, "but I'm not sorry about the rest of it. I'm glad you agreed to have dinner with me. And I'm glad to finally know what's been going on all this time. Maybe the three of us can go out later this week when he's feeling better."

His words made her heart light with a sense of hope she'd been lacking all these years. His cool response to finding out about Joey had worried her that he would remain hands-off. "That would be nice."

Xander placed a palm against her cheek, stroking her soft skin before leaning in to press his lips against hers. This wasn't like the kiss in the parking lot. That one had left her achingly unfulfilled and burning for his touch. This kiss was tender, comforting, and it warmed her body and soul.

"May I have a word?" Craig's sharp voice cut through the moment, causing Xander to jerk away. He looked at her brother for a moment and then he nodded.

"What's this all about, Craig?" Rose asked.

Craig crossed his arms over his chest. "I just want to have a chat with Xander."

Rose planted her hands on her hips and scowled at her brother. He'd always been an overprotective bear. She appreciated the role he played in Joey's life—that father he didn't have until now—but she didn't need his two cents on this situation. And she certainly didn't want him giving Xander a good talking-to.

"I don't think that's necessary," she said. "You're not my daddy."

"Daddy would do it if he were here. This talk is ten years overdue."

Rose opened her mouth to argue, but Xander held out his hand. "It's okay. I don't have any problem talking with Craig. It'll be fine."

Rose scowled at her brother and swung her purse over her shoulder. "Fine, but there'll be none of that stepping-outside nonsense. If you've got something to say to him, you'll say it while I'm standing here or not at all." She could see some of her brother's bravado dissipating. He couldn't be the macho jerk he wanted to be while she watched and Rose knew it. "Go ahead," she said, her tone sharp. "Say what you've got to say, Craig."

Craig took a deep breath and turned to Xander with a frown. "Fine."

"Before you start," Xander said, "I wanted to say thank you."

That brought Craig's rant to a sudden stop. "You want to thank me?"

"Yes. Apparently, a lot has happened while I've been gone. I wish I had known the extent of it, but I can't go back and change things now. So thanks for being there for Rose and Joey. She told me how you take him to games and practices. It means a lot to me to know that Joey wasn't missing out because I wasn't a part of his life."

Craig's square chin tipped up as his chest puffed. "You're right," he said. "He hasn't missed out. I've done everything I can to make sure of it. He's a happy kid. He knows he has family that loves him. I'm not going to let you waltz in here and hurt him."

"Craig!" Rose chastised, but her brother ignored her.

"No. It needs to be said." He pointed his finger at Xander but stopped short of touching him. "If you're going to be in his life, you can't half-ass it. No announcing you're his daddy and then hightailing it back to D.C. and forgetting about him for months at a time. That's not how it works."

Rose held her breath. Xander was a busy man with a schedule that didn't leave time for much, especially the obligations of a child. They hadn't talked about this yet. There were a lot of things still to discuss, but she worried if Craig pushed too hard, Xander would walk away from the whole thing. At this point, she couldn't prove Joey was his child. He was taking this on what she told him and what his eyes perceived.

"You're absolutely right," Xander said, and the air rushed from her lungs. "You can be certain that Joey will be our number-one priority as Rose and I work this out. This isn't something that can be resolved in a night. And for now, we've agreed not to tell him about me yet. Or tell anyone, for that matter. I'd appreciate it if you would help keep this secret until we're ready."

Craig seemed to follow along in agreement, but when Xander finished, her brother tensed up and eyed him with suspicion once again. "Sometimes I forget you're a politician. This all sounds real good, but I can't believe a word you say. I'll keep this secret for Joey's sake, not yours. You've got to prove to me with actions, not words, that you mean what you say."

"I'll do everything I can to prove to them, and to you, that I mean it." Xander offered his hand to shake on it.

Craig accepted it, but before he let go, he leaned in and said something else Rose couldn't hear. Xander stiffened slightly at the quiet words, and then he nodded and pulled his hand away. Whatever the discussion, it seemed to satisfy her brother.

"Night, Rose," Craig said, heading out to his truck with a casual wave. "I'll pick you up about ten for work."

Rose just shook her head. She would never understand men. She watched Craig drive away and glanced at her watch. Great. He'd be back in about six hours. Who needed sleep? It was highly overrated.

"I'd better go," Xander said. "Do you need anything else tonight?"

She turned to him and sighed. "No. You've done enough, thank you. I'm sorry about my brother. He's not very sensitive to how all this must be for you."

"Don't be sorry," he said. "If my sister was in this position, I'd probably do the same thing. Only I'd have my three brothers and Ken scowling behind me."

"I'm surprised Julianne can date at all." Rose could barely stand one overbearing brother. How Julianne managed with all four of the Eden boys and her father watching, she didn't know. Last Rose had heard, Julianne hadn't married yet, either. Maybe the brothers were successful.

Xander smiled, confirming her suspicions. "If she does, she's smart and keeps quiet about it." He took a step toward her and wrapped his arms around her waist. Rose allowed herself to be pulled against him, the protective cocoon of his body welcome after a long, distressing night. He dipped his head to kiss her again. Reluctantly, he pulled away and took a step toward the door. "See you soon, Rose."

After the door shut, Rose let her body sink back against the wall. A swirl of emotions in her gut, compounded by exhaustion, made it hard for her to keep herself upright.

The future was wide-open now and she had no idea what to expect. It scared the hell out of her.

* * *

If you hurt my sister or my nephew, I swear I'll be sharing a cell with my dad that very same day.

Those were Craig's exact words, yet they'd inspired more confusion in Xander than fear. The threat was clear and Xander understood how concerned Craig was with keeping Rose and Joey happy and safe.

But a cell with his dad? Admittedly, Xander was out of touch, but certainly he would've heard something if Billy Pierce was in jail. Right?

There was only one way to find out for certain. Xander rolled out of bed sometime around lunch that afternoon. He got dressed and made his way from the converted barn known as the bunkhouse, where he and the other boys stayed growing up, over to the main house to talk to Ken or Molly.

He opened the back door, walking straight into the old kitchen he'd raided repeatedly during his teen years. His foster father, Ken, was sitting at the worn kitchen table, hovering over a bowl of soup and crackers.

"Morning, son," Ken said, looking up and then back down at his watch. "Good afternoon, rather."

"Hi, Dad."

"Grab some soup and join me."

"Sounds good." Xander went to the stove, where beef-and-vegetable soup was simmering in a large pot. Even though it was only Ken and Molly on the farm now, she still cooked as if she had a houseful of teenage boys to feed. He ladled soup into a bowl and took it and a glass of tea with him to the table. "Where's Mom?"

"She went into town to the farmers' market. Everyone is getting ready for the strawberry festival this weekend. She wanted to pick up a bushel or two of Joe Wheeler's berries and plan her entries for the baking competition."

Every summer, Cornwall hosted the Strawberry Days Festival. Friday, Saturday and Sunday would be filled with parades, carnivals, food booths and contests. Someone would be crowned Queen of the Berries. Molly would cook herself half to death this week in the hopes of bringing home one of the coveted blue ribbons. The most cut-throat of competitions were the strawberry-preserves and the strawberry-pie categories, and the winner could lord it over all the other women in town the rest of the year.

Xander could remember eating so many of Molly's practice dishes as a kid that he went nearly two years in college without eating strawberry *anything*. He swallowed a spoonful of soup and shook his head. Molly worried herself sick every year and never won, even though her stuff was great. "I'm surprised she's still butting her head against that wall. You and I know it's a setup and the mayor's wife always wins. I know corruption when I see it."

"Yes, but she's stubborn, just like all of you kids."

Xander smiled at the incredulity of his father's statement. "You're not including yourself in that group? The man who had a heart attack but refused to tell his kids because it was nothing? The man who'd rather sell off huge chunks of land than admit to his extremely wealthy children that he'd lost his medical insurance and needed some help with bills?"

Ken shrugged. "You all come by it honestly, I suppose."

Xander shook his head and ate his soup. His father had no idea how much trouble he'd caused by selling that land. The unused back portion of the farm had served no purpose to him; it paid off his medical bills without causing a fuss. He couldn't fathom why the kids were so upset. They were upset because they knew what was hidden in the far section of the property.

And now so did the whole town. They just didn't know

who it was. Over the months, the information had been slow to come and sparse when it did. Cornwall didn't deal with many murder victims. So far the only information the police had released was that the remains had been buried for approximately fifteen to twenty years and that it was the body of a young adult male.

When they'd found out Ken had sold the land, Xander's oldest brother, Wade, had come home to deal with the issue and buy back the land before anything could happen. Unfortunately, their parents had sold three plots and Wade had secured the wrong one. They hadn't found that out until the body was found on another piece of the property.

Then the dead man's sister had come to Cornwall looking for answers about her missing brother. Brody had sounded the alarm and dug up a mountain of information they could use against her if necessary. So far it hadn't been needed. There was no information on her brother to find. Everyone had told her what they knew—Tommy had run away from his foster home a week before his eighteenth birthday and had never been seen again.

Now that Congress was out of session and the facial re-creation sketch could hit the news at any moment, it was Xander's turn to deal with the potential fallout. An entire situation that could've been avoided if Ken hadn't been so pigheaded.

Of course, if none of this had happened, Xander wouldn't have known he had a son. Everything was a mess, but somehow he couldn't regret that.

"What kept you out so late?" Ken asked. "Molly said you were going to that new Italian place, but they close at eleven. I heard your car roll in close to four this morning." His bright blue eyes looked over his son, waiting for his explanation for the five-hour gap, as if he were seventeen and out past curfew again.

"I had to take my date to the hospital."

Ken's eyes widened in surprise, his cracker hovering halfway to his mouth. "Go that well, did it?"

"It wasn't her," Xander said with a smile. "Her son broke his arm and we had to meet him there." Xander was surprised how hard it was for him to say "her son." It hadn't even been twenty-four hours since he uncovered the truth and yet Joey was already "his" in his own mind.

He wanted to tell Ken the truth, but it was too soon. He couldn't tell Ken and not let him tell Molly. That would put him in a bad place with his wife. Molly was desperate for grandchildren. If she was the last one to find out that she had one—and he was ten—someone would get hurt. "You remember Rose, don't you, Dad?"

"Your high school girl?"

"Yeah."

Ken nodded. "Sure. I saw her at the diner a few weeks back. Is that who you went out to dinner with? Your mother didn't know."

"I didn't tell her, but yes, I had dinner with Rose. I didn't want Mom to read too much into it."

"I forget that she has a son," Ken added. "I've never even seen her with him, but they live a few towns over, I think."

"He's a cute kid. Broke his arm pretty bad on the trampoline."

"That's a shame," Ken said, pushing aside his empty soup bowl. "That whole family has faced one stroke of bad luck after the other. First Billy's wife got that awful cancer. Things were so hard for them after that. He nearly ran their auto shop into the ground, he was so lost without her. And then…well, it's no wonder Billy got wrapped up in that bad stuff."

Xander's ears perked up. He knew his parents would

know what was going on with Rose's father. Molly knew everything that happened in this town, and whether Ken cared or not, Molly would tell him all about it. "Bad stuff?"

"I forget you guys miss out on everything going on around here. About five years ago, Billy got in with the wrong crowd. He was recruited to drive the getaway car while a couple of them robbed a bank."

Xander felt his soup start to churn in his stomach. He'd known that Billy being in a cell didn't bode well, but he'd hoped for check fraud or tax evasion. A crime, but one that didn't hurt anyone. He'd never anticipated armed robbery.

"Billy just sat in the car and drove off when they ran out. He had no clue what actually happened inside the bank, but apparently, things went badly. One of the guys shot and killed a security guard. It was a big mess."

Yes. Yes, it was a big mess. Xander tried not to outwardly react, but the universe seemed to be conspiring against him. He'd managed to avoid scandal all this time. Now he had enough circling around him to end his political career forever.

Illegitimate children, murder, armed robbery—it was getting downright juicy. Heaven forbid one of the news outlets got ahold of this. If all this was so easily uncovered, he couldn't imagine what a determined reporter could find if he really tried. On the bright side, he'd have plenty of fodder for a second book if all this didn't tank the first one.

Xander wouldn't lie. He wanted Rose. Badly. Before she got that call, he was pretty certain he'd been on the verge of having her. Her cheeks had been flush, her lips bee-stung with kisses. She'd been pressing against him and making those soft sounds of desire that he remembered from all those years ago. And then everything fell apart. He still wanted her, but was it even possible now? He'd sensed her pull back after their kiss at the restaurant. She might've just been worried about her son, but it seemed like more than that. As if she regretted it.

And even if that wasn't true, the night had ended far more complicated than it had started. They could try to keep Joey and her father's incarceration a secret, but eventually, word would get out that he was romantically involved with Rose. It wouldn't take much digging for a reporter to find out the rest and start connecting the dots.

And that was just Rose's family. Never mind that Xander was fighting to keep his own skeleton buried. "How did Rose take it?"

"I'm not sure. I know that's when she moved back here with her son. She tried to run her dad's garage for a while, but her brother took over eventually. Molly mentioned that Rose always seemed so positive when she spoke to her. I think she copes by trying to pretend it didn't happen."

"That's probably true," Xander said. "She didn't mention it to me at all last night. That's sort of a big thing."

"You can't blame her. If one of you committed a stupid and violent crime, I wouldn't be shouting it from the rooftops."

Xander swallowed a mouthful of soup and opted not to respond. The last year and a half, he and his siblings had been struggling—not to stay out of jail but to keep Tommy Wilder's death and their involvement a secret from their parents. They'd never wanted or intended to do what they did that day. Their hands had been forced by circumstances and the fear of losing their new home and parents.

But they *had* committed crimes that day. Heath had killed Tommy while trying to protect Julianne. Wade had hidden the body. Xander and Brody were both guilty of destroying or fabricating evidence. Brody had taken Julianne to the bunkhouse to clean up and change out of her torn and bloody clothes. Xander had gathered her clothes and burned them, along with all of Tommy's belongings, and then forged a note from Tommy. Heath had cleaned up the scene.

They were just kids. Hell, Heath and Julianne were only thirteen at the time. They'd panicked and done what they thought they had to do to protect themselves. If pressed, they could prove Tommy's death was an accident that happened while defending their sister from Tommy's attack. Anyone who knew Tommy back then knew what he was capable of. He stole, he got into fights and he didn't do his fair share around the farm. He'd been brought to the Garden of Eden as a last-ditch attempt to find him a foster home when his own family could no longer control him and no one else would take him.

But that didn't mean the truth wouldn't disappoint their parents. That the shock of it wouldn't give Ken another attack or break Molly's heart. At the very least, Ken would beat himself up for being sick that day and unable to protect his young daughter when she needed him. He might feel guilty that his sons had had to do it for him and carried the burden of their actions for all these years.

Xander couldn't disappoint his parents. Or Rose. Or his son. He wouldn't disappoint his constituents or the people who depended on the Fostering Families Center, either. They had put their faith in him and he wouldn't abuse their trust.

It seemed everyone had their secrets. Now Xander just had to make sure these secrets didn't destroy everything they'd worked so hard to build.

Five

Every time the chime on the front door of the diner went off, Rose jumped. She was a nervous wreck. She'd accidently poured water into someone's lap instead of their glass. There were three order mistakes because she'd written them down wrong. Then she botched the apple pie she needed to bake for the dessert case by adding cups of salt instead of sugar.

She had been on pins and needles the past few days waiting for Xander to show back up again. Sunday had been a big night filled with revelations, kisses and confessions. She still wasn't entirely sure how she felt about this whole turn of events. It felt good to get the truth about their son out, but everything else was so confusing.

Their date had been wonderful, and the physical reaction to their kisses too strong for her to ignore. A part of her wanted Xander, even if it would be a short-term arrangement. The other part urged her to keep her distance, physically and emotionally. She was no good at separating the two, as was evidenced by her anxiety over his extended absence. She had been busy taking care of Joey and working, but not so much that she didn't notice he hadn't come around to see her *or* Joey.

Today was Wednesday and she hadn't laid an eye on Xander. Perhaps it was too much for him at once. He'd seemed to take the truth about Joey well. Maybe too well. She'd expected him to be angry at her for lying to him or to accuse her of passing off another man's child as his. Instead his stoic expression had only given away hints of sadness and disappointment, while his words seemed to understand what she'd done and why.

Perhaps that polished politician's facade hid the truth and he was quietly freaking out. Or calling his lawyer.

"Rose, are you ready for the strawberry festival?"

She snapped out of her own head and turned to the older gentleman sitting at the counter. Lloyd Singer owned the local pharmacy. Every day, he closed up shop and had lunch at the diner, sitting on the very same stool at the bar. He always ordered a Coke with light ice, a patty melt or a Reuben, and a piece of pie or cake. Today he'd opted for a slice of her strawberry cloud cake. He was a big fan of Rose's baked goods. Pity he wasn't one of the judges this year.

Rose smiled and picked up his mostly empty soda glass. "You know what, Lloyd? I've hardly given it a thought. Is it this weekend?"

Lloyd shook his head. "That's what all the banners hanging over the street say. You know, the big red banners with the white block letters. Pretty hard to miss."

"I've been preoccupied," she admitted, and it was the truth. Between Joey's arm, Craig's macho posturing, Xander's return to Cornwall and receiving another unwanted letter from her father, she'd had zero time to worry about what she was going to make.

"I think," Lloyd almost whispered, leaning in, "you should go with this strawberry cloud cake. I've never tasted anything like it. I'd love to see Lois Walters lose for once." He pointed at his half-eaten dessert with his fork. "This could do it."

That was a good idea. She'd never made that for the festival. The cake category wasn't as hotly contested as some of the others, but the winner of each group did compete for the overall best in show. Wouldn't that be a coup? "I'll keep that in mind, Lloyd. Let me get you a refill."

Rose carried his glass over to the soda dispenser and when she turned around, she nearly spilled the glass, she had such a start. Like a ninja, Xander had slipped into the diner undetected and was now sitting beside Lloyd at the counter, chatting. He was looking incredibly handsome today in a blue polo shirt and khakis. His light brown hair was brushed back out of his eyes and his jaw had a hint of stubble, as though he'd skipped shaving this morning. It was a casual look for him, but she could tell it wasn't cheap. The tiny polo player stitched onto his chest meant it was a Ralph Lauren piece.

He looked more like the Xander of her memories today. Without the suits and ties and expensive accessories, he was just the boy she'd fallen in love with and she was defenseless against his draw. It made her want to reach across the counter and caress his face. Imagining the rough feel of his unshaven jaw along the palm of her hand sent a thrill through her whole body. The mere fantasy caused goose bumps to race across her skin.

What would actually touching him do to her? She knew the answer to that and a part deep inside of her tightened at the thought. She took a deep breath to compose herself and returned with Lloyd's drink as though she hadn't even noticed Xander was there. She didn't want him to think she'd been sitting around waiting for him the past few days.

Or the past eleven years.

"Afternoon, Xander," she said with a polite, blank smile she hoped hid the maelstrom of emotions swirling around inside her. "What can I get you today?"

Xander ignored the menu, glancing briefly at the chalkboard for the specials instead. "The chicken and dumplings and a slice of that pink, fluffy goodness he's got there."

"You got it." She disappeared into the kitchen to put his order in. It came up quickly since Oscar already had it made, so she brought it out a few minutes later with a tall glass of water and a slice of strawberry cloud cake.

Lloyd was gone when she returned. It was the tail end of the lunch rush and most of her customers were settling up and returning to work. She dropped off Xander's food and busied herself collecting dishes, waving goodbye and scooping up the tips into her apron pocket.

When there were no more chores to handle or customers to serve, she returned to her lone customer at the counter. He had finished off his lunch and was halfway through his cake. "Everything okay?" she asked.

Xander nodded. "Give my regards to the baker. This strawberry cake is blue-ribbon material. And since I've been recruited as one of the judges, that really means something."

Rose smiled. "You're one of the judges, huh? Then I probably shouldn't tell you, but I'm the one that baked it."

His brows shot up. "You made this?"

"I do most of the baking here. The owner pays me for each dessert on top of my hourly rate. When I dropped out of college, I got a job working at a bakery near the university. I did mostly counter service, but after a while, I got to help out in the back, too."

"This is amazing. I'm not entirely sure what it is, but it tastes great."

"It's basically a layered angel food cake with a fresh strawberry-meringue filling and iced with white fluff."

"Fluff?"

"A girl has to keep some secrets," she said.

Xander glanced around the diner and then turned back to her. "Speaking of which…" he began, and Rose's heart stuttered nervously in her chest. "I know we had a lot of other things to talk about the other night, but why didn't you tell me about Billy?"

Rose gritted her teeth and turned her head to look out the window to the street. She couldn't face him while she talked about this. It was embarrassing enough. "I thought I was throwing enough crap at you already. You asked me out to a nice dinner to reminisce about old times. I didn't want to burden you with my sob story. On a good day, I can convince myself that my father was killed rescuing drowning orphans or something. Then he writes me a letter and I'm forced to realize he's just a sleazy criminal." Rose sighed. "So who told you?"

"Your brother said something that didn't make sense, so I asked Ken about it."

Stupid small towns. Nothing could happen without everyone knowing about it. Rose rested her elbow on the counter and cupped her chin in her palm. "No wonder you didn't come rushing to see me again. Your illegitimate son's grandfather is a felon serving fifteen to life for conspiracy to commit armed robbery and felony murder. There's a headline you don't want to see going into your campaign."

"That's not why I haven't been to see you," Xander said.

"First, I didn't want to come by so soon and draw attention to us. We agreed we weren't going to tell anyone I was Joey's father. Having me hanging around all the time will eventually give us away. I decided to focus on some different things instead to kill some time until I could come in. My book is coming out tomorrow, so I was doing a lot of phone interviews with radio stations and such. Now that all that's done, I came straight over."

"Really?" Rose asked with a coy smile. She knew she shouldn't be pleased, but knowing he was just waiting to see her again gave her a little thrill.

Xander's green-gold eyes focused on her with nothing but sincerity showing in them. "*Really.* I'd like to take you out again."

"The diner is closed this weekend for the festival. Daisy's owner usually pays for me to enter the bake-off because it's good advertising for the restaurant if I do well. When I'm not doing that, I'll have Joey with me. I promised him that we'd go to the fair and watch the parade. With his arm, I'm not sure he can ride anything, but I'll load him up with funnel cake and cotton candy."

"That sounds great. I've got to spend a couple hours Friday judging the bake-off, but do you mind if I join you at the fair? Maybe the parade, too, on Saturday?"

Rose sputtered for a moment, surprised that he was interested. It was one thing to take her to a clandestine dinner in another county. Going to the big town event together was another matter altogether. "Well, of course, I mean, yeah, if you want to. I guess I thought…"

"Thought what?"

"I thought that you might not want to be seen in public with Joey. Just in case someone noticed the resemblance."

Rose could tell that Xander hadn't thought of that. He got that distant look in his eye as he considered it.

"I think it will be okay," he said. "I instantly recognized the younger version of myself in Joey but others, especially the people that didn't know Heath and I as children, might not see it. Some folks might've forgotten that we even dated. They'd have no reason to think anything of it."

"Are you sure?"

"Yes. I want to spend time with you and Joey. I don't intend the process of getting to know my son to be a covert affair. Or spending time with you. There are some things that have to be kept secret for now, but that's not one of them."

Rose was stunned nearly speechless. He had taken the news of his parenthood well, but she'd been certain he would want to maintain his distance. It was her idea to keep the story quiet and she had been counting on it to hold her hormones in check. This was a complicated situation with an expiration date. The distance would help her keep that in perspective, since none of that mattered to her when he was close. Or touching her. But if he wanted to spend time with her and their son, she would be a fool to tell him no.

"Then you're welcome to join us. I'm sure Jocy will get a kick out of it. Maybe you can win him one of those stuffed animals. I'm no good at those midway games and with his arm, you're our only hope."

Xander smiled wide. "I've still got a pretty good pitching arm. I'll see what I can do. Anyway, what I lack in skill, I can make up for in cash."

Xander flipped off the television as he did each night after the news. Another day had gone by without the damning facial re-creation hitting the airwaves. He was beginning to think that maybe Brody was wrong. Brody could've gotten information about them planning to do one, but then they changed their minds or it got delayed. Xander didn't want it to come out, but he was here to deal with the aftermath. This was his longest break of the year—his summer vacation of sorts.

When Congress went back into session, it would be solid work through to Christmas. If something hit then, there was very little he could do about it.

He decided to log into his computer and send Brody an email. Maybe he had an update on what was happening. He sat patiently as hundreds of emails loaded into his inbox. Xander had kept up on his phone, but he hadn't been on his laptop in a couple of days.

He'd been spending time working on the farm with Ken. It had been years since he'd done that kind of thing. It felt good to get out there on the riding mower, trim and shape the trees, and check for any infestations. After spending a good part of the past eleven years at a desk studying or at a desk working, it was a welcome change. Pine trees weren't nearly as frustrating as the bipartisan committees he worked on.

The last of his email was loading when an icon popped up on his screen with a video-chat invitation from his younger brother, Heath. Xander accepted and the window opened, connecting them and activating his webcam. At last his screen refreshed and the ever-unflattering image of his brother popped up. How people dated online with these things, he'd never know. Everyone looked ridiculous on a webcam.

"Evening, little brother," Xander said.

"Hey," Heath replied. He appeared to be using his laptop in bed. Xander could see the padded leather headboard behind him. "I'm glad I caught you online. I haven't seen you active very often lately."

"Well, you know how things are up here. Dad's got me mowing the fields."

Heath laughed. "And they wonder why we moved away and don't visit often. Most kids outgrow chores, but not farm kids."

"It's just as well. Mom's feeding me like I'm seventeen again. If I don't do some manual labor, I'll have to drop a couple grand to get my suits let out. So what's going on?"

Heath's face grew slightly more serious, which was not its normal state. His brother was the funny, easygoing one. He was always quick to make a joke in a tense moment, but there wasn't much joking to be done when the topic of Tommy Wilder came up. "I was wondering if anything had come out about the sketch."

His younger brother had the most to lose if the truth came out. It was justified, one hundred percent, but when it came down to it, Heath had killed Tommy. How a scrawny thirteen-year-old boy had gotten the best of a hulking nearly eighteen-year-old menace, Xander would never know. Heath was scrappy, but Tommy was a dangerous physical presence. Only Heath and Julianne had been witnesses to Tommy's death and neither of them had ever wanted to talk about how it had happened. He didn't blame them. Everything the other kids had done was to protect them both from what they'd had to face.

"Nothing yet. I actually got onto the computer tonight because I wanted to check with Brody to see if he had any more information. There hasn't been a peep about the body the whole time I've been here. No one has even mentioned it." With everything that was going on with Rose, sometimes Xander even forgot why he was in Cornwall to begin with.

His brother sighed with relief, but then his expression changed to one of curiosity. Heath's light eyes, so much like his own, squinted at the screen, his nose wrinkling in thought. "What else is going on?"

Xander sat up straight and shook his head dismissively. "Nothing is going on. Like I said, it's been quiet."

"No," Heath said. "You've got that look on your face. You're lost in your thoughts and your right eyelid keeps twitching. You haven't told me everything."

"There's nothing to tell about the situation with Tommy," Xander insisted.

"And what about things that don't have to do with Tommy, Mr. Lie By Omission?"

Heath knew him too well. His brother could tell he had things on his mind. And he wanted to tell him. He needed someone to confide in. Since Heath wasn't in Cornwall and wouldn't be anytime soon, he might be a safe choice.

"Okay," Xander said, "but when I tell you that this is a secret, I mean it. You can't tell Brody or Wade or Julianne. Not Mom or Dad. No one. I don't even want you telling your chick of the week that I've never even met."

Heath's eyebrows went up. "Wow. This must really be good. I won't tell."

"I mean it, Heath. You can't breathe a word to anyone. No crossed fingers, no writing it down to get around 'telling.' This has to stay secret. I shouldn't even tell you but I need to talk to someone."

"I swear that I will not share this information with anyone via any means of communication, including Morse code, American Sign Language and pig Latin. If I so much as breathe a word of it, you can come to my apartment and take a baseball bat to my Super Nintendo system."

That was probably as good as it would get with Heath. Their parents had bought him that Nintendo the Christmas before they died. "Okay. Brace yourself, because this is a big one. I'm a father. I have a ten-year-old son named Joey."

Heath's eyes grew wide on the screen. He did some math on his fingers. "Rose?" he asked.

Xander nodded. "I just found out."

"Holy crap," Heath said, running his hand over his hair in disbelief. "Have you seen him?"

"Yes. He doesn't know I'm his father, though. Rose and I decided to wait."

"To wait for what? You've already waited ten years."

"It was her suggestion. I don't think she's ready to deal with the town gossip and press scrutiny when it comes out. Neither am I, frankly. It would help if we could wait until after my book tour. Maybe even after my reelection campaign. It's not a huge scandal, but combined with some other factors, it might give my competitor an edge."

"You're going to make that little boy wait a whole year to find out the truth because it might look bad in the papers?"

When he said it like that, it sounded horrible. "I wanted to make it official, but filing any kind of paperwork would send up red flags. I'm used to the press interfering in my life, but they'd swarm all over Rose. She didn't ask for that. Life is different for a politician. We're scrutinized for every little thing."

"So what? You weren't caught in a public restroom with an underage transvestite hooker."

Xander sighed. "Yeah, but I'm the face of the Fostering Families charity. I spend all my time preaching the virtues of taking in needy children. I wrote a book on it. How would it look if it came out that I had a child I'd abandoned?"

"How can you abandon a child you didn't know about?"

"Somehow the press would find a way to hang me for it. By the time the truth came out and everything blew over, it would be too late to undo the damage. If my book tanks, Fostering Families won't raise the money they need. If I'm not reelected, I no longer have the platform to help them. They can't survive without my support. Even if I decided I didn't care about being reelected and I chose to move back to Cornwall and work on the farm, I couldn't let the people at the center down."

"You're not the only person responsible for keeping that charity afloat. It doesn't rest solely on your shoulders."

"It feels like it. I just need some time. Time to spend with Rose and Joey without the press breathing down my neck. Time to figure out how to handle this. I might be able to spin the whole situation in a way that won't hurt my public image, long-term."

"You worry too much about what people think. You're just like Jules that way."

"I have to worry. I'm on a career fast track, Heath. The party has a lot of faith in me and my future. There's been talk…" His voice faded out. He hadn't mentioned this to anyone before; he didn't want to jinx it, but it mattered. "There's talk about me being a major force in the party someday. I'm being groomed for bigger and better things. This might not be a big deal for a small-potatoes congressman no one has ever heard of outside his district, but that kind of visibility leads to higher scrutiny. Would I ruin my chances with a secret love child? Will the House elect a Speaker with that background? Would the public elect a president whose First Lady has a father in prison? I don't want any of this to get out until I know how I want to handle it."

"First Lady?" Heath perked up. "Prison? Back it on up. Start with the First Lady thing. That's a pretty big leap to take. Are you guys serious? You haven't even mentioned her in years."

"No, we're not serious. We've been on one date." Somehow it felt like more than that, though. As if the years they were apart were just a heartbeat in time. He had to fight to keep reality in perspective. And his hands off of her when they were together. "Yeah, I'm attracted to her. She's even more beautiful than I remember. Being with her again felt…like old times. Like I was almost a teenager again. I want to see more of her. I don't know what 'more' entails, but considering she's raised my son alone all these years, marrying her might be the right thing to do."

"Wow, you romantic, you! Just what a girl wants to hear."

"You know what I mean! I would've done it eleven years ago if she had let me. I guess that's why she kept quiet."

Heath sat silent on his computer screen for a moment before throwing out the big question. "But do you love her?"

"I did once. I very well might again. I know I've never loved anyone else. I've regretted letting her walk out of my life, and knowing the truth, now I regret it even more. I know I care about her and I care about our son. I don't want him to be embarrassed about how he grew up."

Heath took it all in with a curt nod. "As usual, you have everything very thoroughly thought out. I'm sure you'll know what to do and things will work out for the best. Just don't do something crazy and elope. Eloping is *always* a bad choice. It's typically born out of a spur-of-the-moment idea, which is usually poor judgment in retrospect. It's a heck of a lot easier to get married than it is to get divorced."

Xander almost wanted to laugh at the sage words of his brother. "You speak like an expert in poor judgment."

"Learn from my mistakes, bro. I am a master of rash decision making. Believe me when I tell you that if you were to elope and Mom finds out, she will strangle you with the ribbon she uses on her Christmas wreaths. Just picture that anytime you think of running off and not including her in it."

"Thanks. That wasn't my plan, but I'll be sure to keep that disturbing image in mind."

"You're welcome. Now what's this about Billy in jail?"

Xander sighed and set his laptop on the coffee table. "Hold on," he said. "I need to get a drink first." He went over to the refrigerator and pulled out a bottle of his favorite beer. If nothing else, it would make telling the story easier. If he'd known he was going to spill his guts to his brother, he would've gotten a drink when they first started talking.

With an open bottle, he returned to the couch and found that Heath, too, had an adult beverage. "I figured if you needed a drink to tell me, I needed a drink to hear it."

"Fair enough." Xander took a large sip and relayed everything Ken had told him about Billy's brush with the law. When he was finished, Heath just shook his head.

"You're a good person, so I just have to conclude that you're being punished for evil deeds in your past life. There's no other explanation for it."

"Tell me about it. I've spent my whole life trying to keep my nose clean. I've always said that the best way to avoid a tabloid scandal is to not do anything scandalous. It's worked so far, but now it's like a pitcher is lobbing fastballs at me quicker than I can hit them."

"Well, at least Rose might be more understanding about the Tommy thing given her father's situation."

At that, Xander laughed out loud. "Oh, no. She is not happy with Billy. Not at all. I don't even know if she goes to visit him. She has no sympathy for him or any other criminals."

"Do you really think of us as criminals?" Heath asked.

Xander shook his head. "No, but that doesn't mean that isn't how other people will think of us. Especially Rose. No, I definitely don't want any of our problems to get back to her. I'll deal with issues as they arise, but I'd be just as happy for her to never even hear the name Tommy Wilder."

Heath finished off his beer and set it aside. "I know it sounds stupid after all of this, but try to enjoy your time there. Get to know your son.... *Man,* it's weird just to say that. I'm an uncle!" he declared, as though he'd just made that connection. "*Uncle Heath.* Ugh. That sounds wrong. We'll have to work out something better. Anyway, spend time with him, visit with our folks. Make the most of your vacation. Don't let all the drama ruin it."

"I'll try," Xander said. It would be hard, but he would try.

"Well, I'd better wrap this up, so let me leave you with this one last thought. Maybe it will make up for the homicidal-mom thing," Heath added with a grin. "If and when you become a political hotshot, it will be in like twenty years. Twenty years from now, your secret love child will be *our age.* Your jailbird father-in-law will be paroled and in a nursing home. Even this crap about Tommy will be a distant memory."

It was hard to imagine, but he was right. Twenty years ago, he was a happy, normal kid living the average American life. How many things had changed since then that he'd never even dreamed of? That many more would change in the next twenty years. When he thought of it that way, it felt like a lifetime away.

"Don't plan your whole life around things that might not matter to anyone down the road," Heath said. "You might miss out on the good things happening now."

Six

Xander was having flashbacks of Molly's test recipes. Even with only a bite or two of each dish, he was overdosing on the red fruit. In the past two hours, he had tasted countless strawberry pies and strawberry cakes. Then came the strawberry-dessert open category, where he sampled strawberry cobblers, strawberry cookies, strawberry ice cream, strawberry gelatin molds and strawberry pretzel salad. His only reprieve was the jams-and-preserves category, the last group, where he could finally have some crackers to kill the cloying sweetness coating his tongue. If he ever got roped into this again, he was going to demand a savory strawberry category to break up the sugar. He had a sweet tooth, but even he had his limits.

There was still some scoring and tallying to do, but when he got out of here, he was marching to the nearest food booth and shoving a mustard-coated corn dog down his throat. He might follow it with some popcorn. Or a soft pretzel. Anything without strawberries.

Xander marked his score on the last jelly and the group took a half-hour break while the scores were being tallied. After that they would choose the best in show from the four category winners.

Now was his chance to drink some black coffee, stretch his legs and perhaps go in search of some salty potato chips in a nearby vending machine.

Aside from the sugar high, it hadn't been too bad. A couple pies were excellent. Rose's cloud cake got his highest score in that group, but only because it really was the best cake he tasted. His favorite jelly had been a spicy strawberry-jalapeño combination he'd never had before, although he wasn't sure if it was really that good, or if he liked it just because it wasn't that sweet.

He had no idea what Molly entered this year, and that was fine by him. He didn't want to know. He'd either feel obligated to give her a good score because she was his mother or obligated to give her a bad score because she was his mother and he didn't want to seem biased. Each dish had been assigned a number, so that was all he knew.

It was nearly seven on Friday night when he was finally cut loose from his judging duties. The winners would be announced tomorrow and would be featured in the parade, but for now, he was a free man.

He texted Rose and met up with them on the far side of the fairgrounds. She and Joey were sitting at one of the picnic tables eating a funnel cake with strawberry topping and whipped cream.

Rose was looking casual but beautiful tonight. She wore a fitted pair of dark denim jeans and a silky off-the-shoulder top in swirls of blue and green. Her long dark hair was braided and wrapped around into a bun. It showcased the long, graceful line of her neck, like a swan reaching up into the moonlight. The blinking carnival lights gave her skin a peachy glow and her lips looked as sweet and juicy as the berry they were celebrating. That was one dish he would gladly overindulge in.

"Hey, everyone," he said, coming up behind them.

Rose turned to him and smiled brightly. He leaned in to give her a brief hug, forcing himself to pull away although he didn't want to. He'd prefer to press her soft body against his own and give her a hello kiss that would leave them both panting, but he wasn't ready for the town busybodies to start speculating on what was going on. That meant it was friendly in public and nothing more.

"Hi, Xander!" Joey said brightly with red goo in the corners of his mouth. He was dressed similar to Xander, with a pair of worn jeans and a T-shirt, although Joey's had Angry Birds on it and Xander's was a plain dark green that Gucci had featured heavily this season. "You want some funnel cake?"

He tried not to groan outwardly. Not even if it were slathered all over Rose's naked body. Well, maybe then.

"No thanks, kiddo." He said the words realizing his father had called him that when he was little. He'd forgotten until he heard himself say it. That made his chest tighten with a wave of emotions he didn't expect. "I've had my fill of sweets for the year. Seen anywhere a guy can get a hot dog?"

"That stand over there has them," Rose said as she pointed to a booth a few yards away.

"Great. I'm going to grab one. Either of you want something? A corn dog? Chili dog? A drink?"

"We could probably use something that isn't sweet, too. You want a hot dog?" she asked their son. "Or would a corn dog be easier with one arm?"

"A corn dog and a lemon-lime soda," Joey said, his mouth still stuffed with funnel cake.

"The same is fine for me. Do you need any help?"

Xander shook his head. "I got this. I'll be right back."

A short line had formed at the booth, so Xander queued up and waited patiently for his turn. He didn't pay any attention to who was around him until he got his food and turned to head back to the table. That was when a blonde woman in line reached out to touch his arm.

"Xander Langston. I didn't know you were in town."

It was Christie Clark. Wealthy, popular, snobby Christie Clark. Xander reacted quickly to turn on his campaign face and smiled warmly. "Christie, so good to see you." He was glad his hands were full and he wasn't able to shake her hand or give her the hug she probably wanted.

Christie eyed his tray of food, then let her gaze stray off into the direction he was heading. The moment she spied Rose and Joey waiting on him, a wicked smile curled her too-pink lips. "I see you and Rose have reacquainted yourselves."

"Yes." Xander nodded, trying not to let her read too much into it. "I saw her down at the diner the other afternoon and I asked if she and her son would be interested in going with me to the fair."

"Her little boy is so darling," Christie cooed. "He's become quite the handsome fella. If I didn't know better, I'd say Rose ran out and found your doppelgänger to date after you went away to D.C."

She was good. Too good. Christie wasn't about to outright state that Joey looked like him. No, she was dancing around it, but her meaning was clear. He wasn't going to let her get to him, though. "Can you blame her?" he asked. "I'm a good-looking guy. I'd try to find another one as handsome as me, too. See you around, Christie."

At that, he turned and headed toward the table. People like her were the reason Rose wanted to keep the truth quiet and he didn't blame her. His jaw was flexed tight with irritation, but he tried to choke it down by the time he returned. He didn't want Rose to see him upset. She would get upset.

"Corn dogs for everyone!" he announced cheerfully, placing the tray onto the table. Rose busied herself handing out the wrapped foods, bags of chips and cans of soda. He watched her for a moment and then let his gaze drift back toward the hot dog booth. Christie was gone, and he was glad. He didn't want her snarky self ruining his night out with Rose and Joey.

"Let's eat," Rose said.

Xander sat down at the table beside Rose and tried to focus on his corn dog. They were hot and crispy, so it was easy to get distracted by the food. When he was finished, he turned toward the bright lights of the midway and noticed a booth for face painting. That might be just the thing for tonight. Joey couldn't do a lot of rides or play many games with his newly broken arm. This would give him something he could do. And if a little embellishment helped to disguise their similarities, all the better.

"You know what?" Xander asked.

"What?" Rose replied.

"I think we should get our faces painted. I haven't done that in years. What do you think, Joey? Should we get you done up like Spider-Man or something?"

"That would be cool. I wonder if they'll do Star Wars characters. A Stormtrooper would be awesome."

Xander had to laugh. He was a pretty big fan himself. He actually might have taken Rose to see one of the later prequels in the theater.

"That's a great idea," Rose agreed with a smile.

They gathered up their trash and made their way down the dirt-and-grass path of the midway. Each booth and game that lined the walkway was lit with bright blinking lights and blared loud arcade music. There were games where you knocked over a pyramid of milk jugs with a baseball, popped balloons with darts, threw a ring over a glass bottle or got a Ping-Pong ball into a bowl with a goldfish in it. Each game had prizes on display ranging from the actual goldfish to giant stuffed bears and inflatable electric guitars.

"Look at that!" Joey pointed to one of the booths. This one required you to flip a quarter and have it land on a series of glass plates without bouncing off. The grand prize was your choice of a huge inflatable baseball about the size of a large beach ball or a pink daisy pillow the size of a trash-can lid.

"You want the daisy pillow?" he teased.

"No!" Joey frowned, making the same pouty face Xander himself used to make. "The baseball!"

"Oh, okay. We'll have to give that a shot after we get painted," Xander said. He had no problem with tossing a handful of quarters away to win that for him. But he wanted the face painting done first so he could breathe easier the rest of the night. "I need to get some quarters. Maybe he'll have some change so you can play."

The face painter had a large wall of samples to choose from. They had a Stormtrooper, but the minute Joey saw Darth Maul, he changed his mind. It took about ten minutes to paint his whole face in the evil red-and-black mask. After that, Rose got a pink-and-purple butterfly and Xander opted for Batman's mask. When they walked out of there, they hardly looked like themselves, much less like each other.

After that, they returned to the midway games and Xander handed Joey a couple dollars in quarters to try and win the inflatable baseball. He and Rose stood back a few feet to watch him play.

"That was very smart," she said quietly after a few minutes. "I'd forgotten how clever you always were."

Xander frowned and turned away from the game to look at her. The sparkling butterfly flattered her elegant cheekbones, but it couldn't disguise the concern lining her eyes. He hated seeing that expression on her face. He wished he could kiss her until she lost her breath and forgot all about her worries. "I guess I wasn't as subtle as I thought I was."

"Well, I'd seen you talking to Christie Clark. I figured she said something to you since you didn't seem as concerned the other day."

"You know Christie," he admitted without elaborating. "She'd be the first to point it out no matter what. I figured if she noticed the similarities and hadn't seen us together, other folks might see the resemblance as we all walked around. I saw the booth and thought it might be something fun for him to do. And if it made it harder for people like her to piece it together, then fine."

Rose nodded and looked down at the dirt. "We can't paint his face every day," she said softly.

"I know..." Xander began, but was interrupted by loud cheers and applause from the booth ahead of them.

"Mom! Xander! I did it! I won!" Joey yelled, his face bright with excitement.

They immediately ended the conversation, rushing forward to congratulate him on securing the giant baseball he'd wanted. Instead of worrying, Xander tried to take Heath's advice and enjoy the moment. He'd always loved going to the fair with Heath and his parents before they died. It was a simple thing, but one he remembered and treasured years later.

To hell with Christie Clark. He wasn't going to lose

these moments because of her smart mouth and smug expression. They were going to have a good time, he was going to enjoy his new family, and he wasn't going to let anyone ruin it.

Even himself.

Around ten the crowds gathered by the small pond near the fairgrounds for the fireworks show. Rose retrieved a blanket from her car and they laid it out to watch the show. The lights were beautiful—she always enjoyed fireworks displays—but it was hard to focus on them with Xander's warm body so close to hers. A few minutes into the show, she felt his fingers seek out hers. No one could see them holding hands, so she let herself enjoy the moment and relished the tingle his touch sent up her arm.

The show ended far sooner than she wanted it to. That meant letting go and returning to reality. After a moment, she reluctantly untangled their hands, sat up and noticed her son was out cold. She ran her hand over his forehead, brushing the sandy strands from his eyes. He didn't even flinch. "I think we wore him out."

Xander sat up beside her. "With all the junk he ate, I'm not surprised. The higher the sugar high, the harder the crash. No problem, though. We'll get him home."

Rose watched him lift Joey with gentle ease. She folded up their blanket and they walked with the crowds back to the parking lots. Xander placed Joey into the back of the car and belted him in.

She'd been amazed at how he'd been with Joey tonight. At first, she'd been worried. It was just like Christie to throw a wrench in their plans. But then it was as if a switch had flipped. Xander seemed to shed his worries like a snake skin and leave them behind. He and Joey had enthusiastically played games and gone through the haunted house. They'd all gotten their pictures taken in the photo booth. He'd even talked the guy manning the swinging pirate ship into letting Joey ride it.

They were little things, but they made a huge difference. She'd never seen Joey's face light up the way it had tonight. It made her very happy to see them together. It also made her incredibly sad that she'd waited so long to bring Xander into Joey's life. It had been the right thing for Xander's career, she was certain of that, and it had saved her the humiliation of begging him to come back for their child's sake, but it hadn't been the right thing for Joey. Craig had done a wonderful job but it wasn't the same.

Xander gently shut the car door without waking Joey. "You should be all set."

Rose looked up at his face illuminated by the overhead lights in the parking field. The shadows played across the sharp angles of his face, making him look handsome and devious all at once. A part of her had broken inside the day she left him, but there was just something about this man she couldn't resist. She wasn't certain if it was the sly smile or the soulful eyes, but she was lost the moment he looked at her. Even with a Batman mask painted on.

"Follow me home," she said quickly before she lost her nerve. She knew that it wasn't the smart choice, but she didn't care. Rose had no doubt that Xander would always be a part of Joey's life. Hers…she needed to take what she could get, while she could. Soon he would return to D.C. and the glamorous women there. Eventually, one of them would be Joey's stepmother. But now, tonight, Xander would be all hers.

"Sure," he said. "I know he'll be hard for you to get out of the car by yourself."

Rose frowned and shook her head. That was sweet, but obviously, she wasn't being clear enough about what she wanted. "Well, yes, but that's not why I want you to come home with me."

His hazel eyes locked on hers as he caught her meaning. He swallowed hard, his jaw tensing. "Are you sure?" he asked.

"No, but it doesn't matter. I want you. If you want me, follow me home."

Xander nodded and took a step back, his expression hard to read. His Lexus was parked on the other side of the field. She watched him walk away, not entirely certain if she would see his SUV behind her or not.

They made their way out onto the highway with the rest of the crowd. Rose's eyes kept darting nervously into her rearview mirror as she drove, watching for his steady headlights behind her. When they passed the turnoff for him to head back to the farm and he was still there, her heart started pounding frantically in her chest. She wanted Xander, and at least for tonight she was going to have him.

Now her only concerns were about how things had changed. The last time they'd made love, she was a fit and firm young teenager with a flat, bare-able belly you could bounce quarters off of. She had worked hard to keep up her figure over the years, but she'd had a baby. She'd breast-fed. She'd aged. Rose thought she still looked pretty good when she strutted in front of the mirror naked, but there would be no quarter bouncing tonight.

She took a deep breath as she pulled into her apartment complex and parked her car. Xander pulled up alongside her and got out. He shot a wide grin of anticipation at her that made her skin start to flush and her belly tense. Her hands were nearly shaking as she opened the car door. Xander winked before dipping down and hoisting Joey out of the car. They went inside together and got him settled into bed.

Rose pulled off Joey's shoes and tugged down his jeans. He could sleep in his T-shirt and tighty-whities tonight. She did want to get off some of that face paint, though. She got a makeup-removing wipe from the bathroom and gave him a few good swipes. Joey whined and squirmed a little in his sleep, but he didn't wake up. She turned on his white-noise machine and joined Xander back in the hallway.

"You got more of those?" he asked, looking pointedly at the red-and-black-smeared wipe.

"Sure. Come on back." Rose led him to the other side of the apartment, where her bedroom and bath were. He followed her into the bathroom, where she plucked another wipe from the box and handed it to him. "Here you go."

She took another and made quick work of the butterfly paint. When she was done, she noticed Xander still had a good bit that he'd missed.

"Let me help," she said, reaching up to caress his face.

The minute she touched him, she could feel the energy in the room change. Xander's hand reached up to cover her own and his eyes closed as he savored the contact.

"Rose," he whispered.

The word traveled like a caress down her spine. Every nerve in her body came alive in an instant. His other hand moved to her waist, his fingertips grazing over her through the silky fabric of her top. Her blood suddenly seemed warmer in her veins. Her cheeks felt flush. Her breasts felt painfully confined by her bra. Modesty be damned— she wanted to strip off all her clothes to let the cool air-conditioning and his sizzling touch combine across her bare skin.

Xander leaned down and his lips met hers. She melted into him, pressing every soft curve of her body into every hard ridge of his. As he tasted her and let his tongue lei-surely explore, she could feel his fingertips gathering her blouse at the waist of her jeans. She put her arms over her head and he broke away from the kiss long enough to pull the top off.

His eyes raked over her with blatant approval. The extra curves she'd picked up over the years didn't seem to bother him. In fact, they seemed to stoke the fires inside of him like never before. It made Rose bold enough to reach behind her and unclasp her strapless bra. Her pale breasts spilled free, the tight pink tips reaching out for his touch.

Xander groaned softly at the sight, but he didn't reach for her. Not yet. He ripped his own shirt over his head and threw it to the ground first. Her breath caught in her throat at the sight of him. He, too, had changed since she'd seen him last. Her lean baseball player had bulked up over the years. He seemed broader, stronger, more powerful now. His bare chest was like a wall, the muscles etched into stone. A sprinkling of light brown chest hair sprawled across his pecs and then traveled down his stomach. It darkened as it disappeared into his waistband, making her palms itch to reach out and unbutton his fly.

Before she could, he stepped forward, his hulking figure nearly overwhelming her own as he pressed his bare skin against hers. His hands gripped each side of her face and drew her mouth back to his. Rose wrapped her arms around him and tugged him closer until her breasts were crushing against his chest.

Xander growled against her mouth. He moved his hands down her sides and over her hips and caressed the curve of her rear through her jeans. Then she felt his fingertips press against the backs of her thighs and before she knew it, he'd lifted her up. She quickly wrapped her arms around his neck and her legs around his waist so she wouldn't lose contact with his lips.

He carried her out of the bathroom and into her bedroom, where he sat her on the edge of the mattress. Crouching down in front of her, he unfastened and slipped her jeans down her thighs. He pulled off her shoes and tossed her clothes out of his way before he guided his hands back up her bare legs to the lace edging of her panties.

Rose was propped on her elbows, watching his exploration with anxiety. The closer his hot breath got to her aching core, the harder it was for her to breathe. He wrapped his fingertips around the lace and tugged gently until they, too, were gone. Then he pressed against the insides of her knees, opening her thighs to him.

The moment his tongue made contact with her skin, she could no longer watch. Her eyes fluttered shut and her head dropped back. She swallowed one gasp of pleasure, then another, as his mouth moved over her slick skin. One hand closed over her left breast, teasing and pinching gently at her nipple until her hips bucked involuntarily against his tongue.

Even after all this time, he knew just how to touch her. In only a few moments' time, she was on the edge, threatening to go over. "Z…" she panted. "Oh yes, Z."

Her encouragement spurred him on. He moved over her sensitive flesh with renewed enthusiasm and before she could catch her breath, she was gasping and writhing against the mattress. Her release hit her hard, his relentless caresses giving her body no escape from the intensity of it.

He waited until she stilled and then whispered against her stomach. "I love it when you call me that."

Rose watched through hooded eyes as he stood up, slid out of his jeans, then slipped into the condom he'd brought with him. She rolled onto her stomach, inching higher onto the bed, but before she could turn over, she felt the heat of his body pressed along her entire back. The weight flattened her against the mattress. She could feel the firm heat pressing insistently at the back of her thigh and his warm breath at her neck.

With a shiver of desire running through her, she parted her legs, allowing him to slip between them. Rose propped herself up onto her elbows, arching her spine and raising her backside up to him.

Nearly every inch of her body was in contact with his as he moved forward and buried himself inside her. "Oh, Rose," he whispered, his voice wavering in her ear. He placed a searing kiss against her earlobe, then another down her neck and another on the bare curve of her shoulder. On his elbows, he reached beneath her and cupped both breasts in his hands.

A surge of pleasure rushed through Rose's body, her muscles tightening around the length of him. Xander trembled and swore against her shoulder, then moved in her again.

Although Rose faced away from him, she'd never felt closer. She could feel every twitch of his muscles against her skin. Every whisper and prayer that passed his lips danced across her neck. It was like being wrapped in a blanket of him, secure, safe and warm.

And then he started moving faster. Rose gripped frantically at the sheets, pressing back and into his every thrust as she felt the coil of need in her belly grow tighter with each passing moment. She had waited so long to have Xander here, in her bed, in her body, again. It was almost hard to believe this was really happening. Xander. Here. Wanting her as badly as he had before.

That thought was enough for her to finally lose control. The rush of heat and pleasure surged through her veins, her inner core throbbing and pulsating around him.

Rose gasped into her pillowcase, her soft cries soon mingling with the low groans of Xander's release.

After a few minutes of ragged breathing, Xander dropped over to her side and collapsed onto the mattress. Rose rolled back and curled against him. It was such a calm, peaceful moment she could almost fall asleep in his arms just like this.

Then a funny thought struck her. "You know, Lois Walters would have a fit if she found out about this."

Xander propped himself up onto one elbow and looked down at her. "Why, of all the things you could talk about in this moment, are we discussing the mayor's wife?"

"It just occurred to me, inappropriate timing or no, that she would be furious if she knew."

Xander sighed and brushed the damp strands of hair from her face. "Knew what?"

Rose cracked her most wicked of grins. "If she knew that I was sleeping with a judge."

Seven

The light was just beginning to shine dimly through the windows when Xander spoke. "I should go."

Rose groaned in protest and rolled onto her side to look at him. Her hair was tousled and sexy, her dark eyes still slightly glazed with sleep. "You don't have to."

Xander placed a kiss on the end of her nose and swung his legs out of bed. "I know, but I was thinking I needed to be gone before Joey woke up."

Before he could press his feet against the carpeting, the rumble of voices sounded from the living room.

"Too late," Rose said. She lay back against the mattress, stretching long like a cat and yawning loudly. "Joey is an early riser. Thank goodness he's finally old enough to make himself cereal and watch television until I wake up."

"Now what?" Xander asked.

Rose sat up and tucked the sheets under her arms. "We get up, get dressed and have breakfast, I suppose. If we don't act like it's a big deal, he won't think it's a big deal."

"Is he, uh, used to you having men stay overnight?"

Rose's mouth fell open in shock. "No," she said, her tone sharp. "I've never had a man over before."

"I wasn't trying to hurt your feelings," Xander said, reaching his arm across the bed to grip her foot through the blanket. "I don't know how much you've dated while we've been apart or how serious it was. I have no room to talk because I assure you it isn't as many people as I've dated."

She frowned and slipped out of the bed. "Glad to know you haven't been pining away for me all these years." Rose pulled on a robe and disappeared into the bathroom.

Xander just shook his head. He always knew just what to say, unless he was around Rose. Then, somehow, his filter short-circuited and he ended up saying things that ranged from rude to tacky to downright insulting. He started pulling on his clothes instead and was dressed when Rose came out of the bathroom.

"I'm going to make some coffee," she said.

They went out together, following the sound of cartoon chaos as they neared the living room.

"Morning, baby," Rose greeted their son.

Joey turned away from the television to glance at them, and then he smiled when he noticed Xander was there. "Morning. Hi, Xander! You want one of my Pop-Tarts? They're s'mores flavored."

"Hey, kiddo," Xander said. "I'll pass on the breakfast, but thanks for the offer. You save those for you."

Joey shrugged and returned to watching the cartoons on the television.

"That was quite the offer," Rose noted quietly. "Are you sure you want to turn it down? Joey won't share his Pop-Tarts with just anyone. Not even Craig. You must be special."

"I'm honored. I'm just not interested in chocolate-and-marshmallow sludge this early in the morning."

"How about coffee?"

"Yes, please."

Rose poured two mugs of hot coffee and passed one over to him. "Joey," she said, "could you turn it over to the news? I want to see what time the parade is supposed to start."

Joey pouted for a moment and then flipped the channel from cartoons to news. The local guy was talking about the weather, and then the woman gave an update on the festival and parade route. It looked as if it would begin at eleven.

"I know they're announcing the bake-off winners at ten," Xander added, "so we should get down there earlier. I have to go by the farm and change first. I probably need to be there by nine-thirty since I'm helping hand out the awards."

"We'll meet you at the winners' ceremony," Rose said.

Xander had turned away from the television once he had the information he needed about the parade, but the woman's voice caught his attention again.

"…sketch to help the local authorities identify the body found at the Bridgeton Properties site last December."

His face jerked back toward the TV in time for the long-awaited sketch to flash up on the screen. Xander's stomach sank, the coffee turning bitter on his tongue. It had finally happened. The artist's re-creation was looking back at him. All hell was about to break loose.

The woman on the news continued to talk while it was displayed. "The coroner's office reported last year that the victim was a young Caucasian male, approximately age sixteen to twenty-four. Cause of death was believed to be blunt-force trauma to the head. If you have any information about this crime or recognize the person in the sketch, please call the local sheriff's office." A number flashed onto the screen.

"That's just awful," Rose said.

Yeah, that was about what he was thinking. Once the Strawberry Days stuff wrapped up today, he needed to get back to the farm to start running interference.

"You never expect something like that to happen where you live," he commented, and it was true. You certainly never expected it to happen to you, either.

"I don't recognize the sketch. Do you?"

"Nope," he said without turning to look again. And honestly, it didn't look that much like Tommy. If he hadn't known for a fact that the dead guy was his former bunk-house-mate, he wouldn't have connected the dots himself.

"Does it freak you out to know that someone died on your parents' property while you were there?"

Xander shrugged. "Not really. The farm is huge. Any number of things could've happened out there and no one would know it. Besides, it might've happened before Heath and I came there. The timeline window they've given is pretty broad."

"That would creep me out. It's bad enough knowing that there's a murderer running around Cornwall some-where," she said quietly so Joey wouldn't hear. "What if it's someone I know? Someone I trust?" Rose shivered into her robe, pulling the plush fabric tighter around her.

He had been right, he thought drily. Rose would not understand. There would be no explaining it to her, only rationalizing away her argument. "It was a long time ago. Anyone could've stumbled onto the property and no one would know it. Two guys hiking through the area might've gotten into an argument in the woods and one could've offed the other. It could be two people we've never met in our life," he added.

"I suppose," Rose agreed. "Are you hungry?"

"A little. I'd be happy to eat anything without strawberries," he said. There would be plenty of strawberry foods today at the parade. He didn't need more here.

Rose nodded and turned away to the refrigerator. As she opened the door, Xander noticed a flyer that read Scout Camp in big letters at the top.

"Is Joey going to scout camp?" he asked. He'd gone at Joey's age and had loved it. He'd learned how to shoot a bow and arrow, tie a million knots, ride a horse and make art out of macaroni.

Rose raised her finger to her lips to quiet him. They both glanced over at Joey, but he had switched back to cartoons and was paying them no attention. "No. He wanted to go, but I couldn't afford it."

"When is it?"

"It starts on Monday. With his arm, even if I could afford it, they probably wouldn't take him."

Xander could specifically recall seeing a boy with a broken arm when he went to camp. If Troy Williams was still the local scoutmaster, maybe Joey could go. Troy had contributed heavily to Xander's campaign. He could give him a call. Joey would have a good time. And given that the sketch just went public, it might be the best solution. Xander wouldn't be torn between spending time with his son and fielding the press. "They might. We should ask. It might make up for missing out on baseball."

Rose frowned. "Xander, I told you that I can't af—"

"And I told you I was going to help," he interrupted. "And he wants to go. If I can get the scoutmaster to agree to let him go, will you let me take care of it?"

Her lips twisted with thought but she didn't answer.

"Seven full days," Xander added, "without a child underfoot. We could each do what we needed to during the day, then I could come over here after work. Imagine how much trouble we could get into. Imagine how *loud* you could be," he said with emphasis.

Rose's dark eyes met his, the bright flame of desire burning in their depths again. He hated that it would be an eternity before he could touch her again. It would be a welcome distraction with everything that was about to happen. She didn't respond, but she didn't need to.

"I'll call Troy on my way home and see what he has to say. If we can't, we can't. But if Joey can go, I want to take care of it."

Rose kept her distance from Xander at the bake-off celebration. The dishes were anonymous, but if she seemed too friendly with Xander, she had no doubt someone would call foul. She'd never won any of the categories before, so she'd hate to sully it, and Daisy's reputation, by getting embroiled in a small-town baking scandal.

Despite that, she could just picture the look on Lois Walters's face if she did win. Scandal or no, it would be worth it.

She currently sat in the back row with a very bored Joey. He was more interested in the parade and food vendors outside since she'd forced him to leave his handheld game system at home. Fortunately, it was going pretty quickly. Edith Andrews took best-dessert open for her strawberry pretzel salad. A beaming Molly Eden defeated her competitors in the jams-and-preserves category for her spicy strawberry-jalapeño jelly. Then Lois Walters won first place for her strawberry pie, surprise, surprise. Rose had to admit it was a very good pie, but she was over the smug, pudgy woman's face gloating about it all the time.

Last was cakes, Rose's category. She had gotten second and third place before, but when her name wasn't called for either, she felt the twinge of disappointment. Sleeping with a judge hadn't helped at all, she thought with a wry grin just touching her lips and lifting her spirits.

"First place goes to the strawberry cloud cake by Rose Pierce."

At first she didn't react. Had she heard that right? Then Joey nudged her and she leaped up from her seat. The crowd applauded as she made her way up to the stage and was presented with a ribbon by the contest coordinator, Mrs. Shipley.

"Please stay on stage, dear. We're bringing up all the winners for the best-in-show presentation."

Rose nodded and stepped to the side. On the table behind them was a trophy for best strawberry dish of the year. She heard Lois had to have a cabinet built for all her trophies, so she didn't hold her breath. Lois, Edith and Molly joined her on stage for the announcement.

"And the winner of best in show is…Lois Walters and her Berrilicious Strawberry Pie!"

Rose laughed and shook her head. She couldn't be mad about it. At least she got first place in her category, and the owners of Daisy's would be thrilled enough about that. She left the stage after the hoopla and she and Joey slipped out to find some real estate for the parade. They found a shady spot on the route and settled onto the grassy slope with some sodas and a container of popcorn.

"I'm sorry you didn't win, Mom," Joey said.

"That's okay," she said, hugging him to her side. "If I won, it wouldn't be any fun. I'd have to ride in the parade and I couldn't watch it with you."

"And Xander?" he added.

Rose turned to look at her son. He didn't just have his father's soulful eyes. He also had his smarts. Nothing got past him. "I think he will be coming, yes, but you're more important than some silly boy I'm dating. Always."

She didn't date much, but she wanted it to be clear that her son was always the most important thing in the world to her. Her father had always seemed to have other priorities—his grief, his business, his criminal proclivities—and she wouldn't do that to Joey. Even in the worst of her mother's illness, she'd always made Rose feel as though she was the center of her universe, and that was the standard she kept to.

"I like him."

"I'm glad," she said, smiling. She'd always known they would get along like two peas in a pod because they were so much alike, even without ever having met before now. "I think he likes you, too."

"Do *you* like him? I've never seen you smile the way you do when you're with him," Joey noted quietly. "You seem really happy together."

At that, Rose was a little taken aback. The past days had been a change from their normal routine, but had things been that different since Xander had returned to Cornwall? "Am I not happy the rest of the time?"

Joey shrugged. "You're tired. You work a lot. There's not much time for you to relax and enjoy yourself. I don't even remember you going out with anyone more than once or twice. I hope you and Xander can hang out some more."

Rose did, too, but there was a ticking time bomb for this romantic interlude. Joey needed to know that. Xander would always be a part of his life, but not necessarily in hers the way it was now. "Well, Joey, you know he doesn't live around here. He's visiting family. Pretty soon he'll go back to Washington, D.C., and work. I don't think much will come of this."

"You could visit him there."

She wouldn't even allow herself those fantasies. If she did go to D.C., it would be to take Joey for a visit. She would be the awkward third wheel. "I don't know, Joey. We both have different lives. We're not thinking that far ahead. Xander and I are just enjoying being together again after all this time. Did you know he was my prom date?"

Joey wrinkled his nose. "No. Really? Did he buy you one of those flower things?"

"A corsage? Yes. He got one for my wrist in red roses that matched my dress."

"She was the most beautiful thing I'd ever seen in my life," Xander said, appearing from the crowd to join them on the lawn. "When she opened the door in that red dress, I thought I might pass out on the doorstep. The only thing that kept me upright was knowing that your uncle Craig would dump me in the pond if I did."

Rose laughed. Craig would've done something like that, she was certain. He'd been scowling at her the whole evening as she got ready. "Welcome, Xander. I'm surprised they didn't corral you into the parade."

He shrugged, settling down on the grass beside her. "I told them I had plans. I didn't want to ride with Lois Walters anyway."

"That's your own fault," Rose pointed out.

"It was good pie!" he said in his own defense. "I wish it hadn't been hers, but damned if it wasn't the best strawberry pie I've ever tasted."

"At least Molly finally got a ribbon."

"She's still beaming over that. She wanted to beat Lois, of course, but a ribbon is a ribbon. Hey," Xander added, lowering his voice a touch. "By the way, I spoke with Troy earlier."

"Anything interesting come from that?"

Xander smiled, his dimples coming out in full force.

"We are all set. The scout camp has a nurse on-site that will check in with Joey and give him pain medication if he needs it. He'll have to skip some of the more active sports and water activities, but he's welcome to go. I already wrote the check. All he needs aside from clothes and toiletries are a sleeping bag and a few forms filled out."

Rose was thrilled for Joey, yet she couldn't help wincing and shaking her head as he finished speaking. "We don't have a sleeping bag."

"We'll get one this weekend. We have to drive him to the campsite and drop him off by nine a.m. on Monday morning. Pickup is Sunday evening."

He had handled all the details. There was no way Rose could complain. She'd wanted her son to be able to go to this and now he could. "Do you want to tell him?"

"Can I?" Xander said, his expression brightening. When Rose nodded, he shouted to Joey over the oncoming marching band music. The parade would reach them any minute now. "Hey, Joey? Guess where you're going next week."

Their son narrowed his eyes and frowned. "To Uncle Craig's house?"

"Nope," Xander said. "You're going to scout camp for the week."

"What?" Joey said, excitement lighting his eyes. "Really? They'll let me go with the cast and everything?"

"It's all taken care of," Xander replied. "We're going to get you a sleeping bag and some first-class scouting supplies when the parade is over."

After a moment, Joey's enthusiasm waned a touch and his brow knit together in thought. "But wait, Mom, you said you couldn't afford for me to go."

Rose nodded and reached out to ruffle his hair. "Xander was nice enough to pay for it."

"I loved going to camp. I hated for you to miss it."

That was enough to soothe his concerns. He grinned and looked over at a group of people settling nearby. One of the boys was from his ball team and was also going to the camp, Rose recalled.

"Can I go tell Ethan?"

"Sure. Don't wander too far or you'll miss the parade."

Joey leaped up and shot off, the cast only marginally slowing him down. He would probably do fine at camp unless he whacked it on something. "Thank you," she said to Xander while still watching her son.

"You're welcome. I know he'll have a great time. Hey, do you have some paper to write down Troy's number? He wanted you to give him a call to talk over things."

"Sure." Rose reached into her purse and pulled out a notebook and pen.

"Oh," Xander said, and he reached down beside them. He picked a folded piece of paper off the grass and held it up to her. "You dropped this."

Rose instantly recognized it and frowned. She'd forgotten that was in her purse. She took the paper from him and crumpled it into a ball in her hand. "Thanks," she said dismissively.

Her pen was still poised in her other hand to write down Troy's number when she realized he was watching her with a concerned expression furrowing his brow just as Joey's had been a moment before.

"What was that, if you don't mind me asking?"

She sighed and clicked the end of her ballpoint pen. Troy's number was apparently on hold. "This," she said, clutching the ball of paper, "is a letter from my father."

The drawn forehead stayed firmly in place. "Really?"

"Yep. Authentic prison mail. I forgot to throw it away." She held it up to toss it toward the nearby trash can, but

Xander caught her hand and plucked the paper from her fingers.

"Does he write very often?"

"About once every two months or so." After he was first incarcerated the letters had come more frequently, at least once a week. Over the years, they'd arrived further and further apart. That was fine by Rose. She didn't want to receive *any* letters.

"Do you or Joey ever write him back?"

Rose turned away from his appraising gaze to the commotion in the street. The bearers of the Strawberry Days banner went past them, followed by the local veterans' group waving red ribbons on sticks. A crowd had gathered along the streets now, families and friends, children on their fathers' shoulders, and the occasional dog on a leash.

"You know, I remember coming to this festival with my dad once," she said. "He put me on his shoulders like that little girl over there. I was maybe five at the time and at first I was scared that I would fall. But my dad had a hold of me and he said that he wouldn't let anything happen to me. He gripped me so tightly that I forgot I was even up so high. I thought I could see the whole world from up there."

Her gaze dropped to the grass as she fought the tears forming in her eyes. "He lied. My whole life he masqueraded as my protector, when in fact he was the one that hurt me the most."

Xander flattened the ball of paper and scanned over the words she couldn't bring herself to read. "He knows what he did to you, Rose, and he wishes you would write to him. He's so sorry about what happened."

"They're just words, Xander. Nothing he says can change the past. And there's nothing he can do in that medium-security federal prison for the next fifteen years. What's done is done. The man that worked in that bank is dead and his family has lost their future with him. My father did nothing but lie to me and he will never be a part of my life again. He's going to miss his grandson's entire childhood. He hid the problems he was having for years. I can't trust anything he says."

Xander's expression went from concerned to pained. Rose couldn't understand why. It wasn't *his* father in jail. "Everyone makes mistakes, Rose."

"There are mistakes and then there are mistakes that leave people dead and turn you into a criminal, Xander. It was bad enough when we were just poor. He made us into trash. You want to know another reason why I never told you about Joey? It was because I was afraid that was how you'd see us. That even if you knew you had a son, you would be too embarrassed of us to ever become a part of his life."

"Rose, you could never be trash."

Xander reached out and tipped her chin up until she had no choice but to look into his hazel eyes. All these years, she had expected to see rejection and shame there when he found out the truth, but today she was surprised by the warmth and acceptance in his eyes. The heat of attraction. The possibility of more. Joey seemed to think that things between the two of them could last beyond his visit to Cornwall. It was a nice thought, but she refused to bet her heart on that.

"Never."

Eight

There were days when Xander didn't appreciate his brother Brody's computer genius. Usually that was when he was able to uncover personal information about Xander that he'd rather not share. But considering everything going on with the as-of-now-unidentified body on the news, he was happy to have some insider information.

Brody had texted him an hour ago and indicated that they hadn't made any announcements, because there were no credible leads on identifying the body so far. It seemed that most people had forgotten all about the troublesome teen who vanished all those years ago. That was a relief.

The more time Xander spent with Rose and Joey, the more he worried about the truth coming out. There was already a lot on the line—their careers, their father's health, their parents' love. Knowing that he had a son raised the stakes. Joey looked at him as if he was the coolest guy he'd ever met. He never wanted doubt or betrayal to show up in the eyes that were so much like his own.

There was already too much in Rose's eyes. From the first moment they were reunited, and even in the moments of passion they'd shared, there had been a hesitation in Rose. Too much had happened in her life—some caused by him, some caused by other people. And while she was letting some of her barriers down slowly but surely, their discussion about her father yesterday made her stance painfully clear.

Xander's secret would ruin everything. If Tommy's body was identified and the truth came out, the two of them would be through. Hell, he would be lucky if she let him see the son he'd just met. As far as Rose was concerned, he would be criminal trash just like her father. If she could cut Billy from her life, Xander would be even more easily dispatched.

According to Brody, things were still okay. For now. Xander would hold his breath and wait for things to change, but in the meantime, he wanted to make the most of his time with Rose and Joey. He was on his way to pick them up and drive them out to the scout campground. Knowing Tommy hadn't been identified yet would be one less thing lurking on his mind.

As it was, he was waiting for the police to question his parents. He'd told Ken to text him the moment they called or showed up. Sheriff Duke was more inclined to set an appointment than arrive unannounced, especially considering how respected the Edens were in the community. But that didn't mean he wouldn't. Xander was not familiar with the man who had taken over the job a few years back.

Xander slowed to turn into the parking lot of Rose's apartment building. It was a nice enough place, but he intended to find her someplace else and well before the winter weather set in. Her Honda didn't have snow tires or four-wheel drive, after all.

Sitting on his pack on the curb as Xander pulled in was Joey, decked out in his scouting uniform. He was bouncing with energy and excitement. When he spied the car, Joey leaped up and ran into the apartment. By the time Xander had parked and opened the hatch to load up his gear, his son had returned with Rose in tow.

She was looking lovely today. She was wearing a snug pair of jeans that clung to each curve and a tank top that gave just a glimpse of her cleavage along with the smooth, unblemished expanse of her décolletage and arms. Her hair was down, spilling like dark brown silk over her bare shoulders. Rose was a tempting treat he couldn't wait to get a bite of. When she got off work tonight, he had every intention of getting a taste.

Joey ran to him, clutching his new sleeping bag with his good arm. "Hi, Xander!" he greeted him.

"Hey, Joey. Are you ready for camp?" He took the sleeping bag and tossed it inside.

"I am. My friend Ethan is going and we're hoping to share a bunk. I'll have to sleep on the bottom because of my arm, but that's okay with me."

Rose rounded the back of his SUV with Joey's backpack. "You're going to have a great time. But you remember to take it easy on that arm. The nurse will have your pain pills if you need them."

"I know," Joey said with an exasperated look on his face. It was obvious Rose had given him this speech several times since they'd found out Joey could go.

Xander slammed the hatch closed. "Let's hit the road, then. Camp Middleton, here we come!"

They loaded into his SUV and hit the highway. It took about thirty minutes to reach the camp and they arrived at the peak of drop-off time. There were scouts and parents everywhere. They checked Joey in and Rose turned over his medication and signed a few waivers for the nurses. The nurse even came to introduce herself to them and pointed out to Joey which of the log cabins had her office in it. A couple older scouts who served as counselors collected his things and carried them to his bunk. Finally, they were shooed over to the Welcome to Camp Middleton sign for pictures.

"This should be just the two of you," Xander argued, but Rose ignored his protests and tugged him into the shot.

"You have to be in it, Xander!" Joey said.

Posing like a real family, they waited for the photographer to snap their picture and the check-in process was finally complete. A few of the counselors were standing several feet away with lettered flags for each of the cabins. The closest flag had an *A* on it for the boys assigned to cabin A.

"There's your group," Xander said. "But one last thing, first." He squatted down and pulled a thick black Sharpie from his back pocket. "This is for all your new friends to sign your cast."

"Thanks, Xander. This is great!" Joey stuck the pen in the pocket of his khaki shorts and rushed forward to give him a hug.

Xander braced himself for impact but underestimated the emotional punch that came with it. He had carried Joey to bed unconscious, given him high fives, ruffled his hair but hadn't actually hugged him. It was the first time he'd held his son in his arms. A wave of feelings surged through him and in that moment, he didn't want to let go. But he knew he had to. "Have fun!" He choked down the emotions and broke into his wide practiced smile.

Joey pulled away with a grin and turned to his mom. Rose gave him a big hug and kiss and then let the squirming boy run off to join the others.

Xander took her hand and led her back to the SUV. "Are you okay?" she asked as they reached the car, surprising him.

"Me? I was going to ask you the same thing."

"I'll be fine. He's getting older and wants to do more things on his own. I've had years to prepare for this, but I saw the look on your face when he hugged you. You seemed a little overwhelmed."

Xander nodded and they climbed into the car. "Things just got a little real all of a sudden."

He pulled out of the gravel parking lot and set a course back to Torrington. In the silence of the drive, Rose reached over and took his hand. He wrapped his fingers through her own and instantly felt better. Rose always seemed to understand the things he kept inside. Back in school, he never had to tell her he was upset. She would just sit down beside him, take his hand and offer her silent support. She didn't push him to talk or layer on empty platitudes to make him feel better.

Rose was just there for him. Then, like now. In the world of politics, that was a rarity. Everyone he interacted with on a daily basis wanted something from him. They were fair-weather friends who could turn on him as quickly as public opinion. His family members were the only people he could count on. They were the ones who would quite literally help him hide a body.

And even though he didn't always deserve it, Rose was someone else he could count on. And he wanted to be there for her and their son, as well. To start, he wanted to spend the next few days getting to know Rose again. She wasn't the teenager he'd fallen in love with anymore. She was more.

Unfortunately, they couldn't just lie in each other's arms all week. She had work. He had to travel to D.C. in a few days for a charity fund-raiser and book signing. Of course, he also had the police to worry about, but he would make the most of the time they had.

He knew Rose had to work today, so he planned to spend time on the farm and meet her later. "What time did you want me to come by tonight?"

"Nine-thirty, maybe? That will give me a chance to get home and get out of my uniform."

Xander glanced over at her with a wicked smile curling his lips. The tank top highlighted the curves he'd touched only a few days ago, and yet it felt like years. "I can help you out of your uniform."

Rose laughed. "I bet you can."

"Shall I bring some takeout with me? Or do you eat at work?"

"You can bring dinner if you want to. I got burned out on the diner food a long time ago. I usually eat something light when I get home. There's a pizza place not far from my apartment complex."

"Pepperoni and green peppers?" he asked. That had always been her favorite in school.

Rose smiled and nodded. "You remembered."

Xander's eyes stayed focused on the road. Somehow it was easier to say the words that way. "The night we broke up, you told me to go off to school and forget all about you, but I didn't. How could I possibly forget about you, Rose?"

Rose didn't respond, but he heard her sharp intake of breath just before his cell phone chirped. The highway was clear, so he glanced down briefly at the incoming text. He sighed when he saw the message from his brother. One more thing to take away from their time alone together.

"When is your next day off?" he asked.

"Wednesday," Rose said. "Why?"

"I just got a text from my brother Wade. He wants to go to dinner this week."

"That sounds nice. I'm sure you'll have fun."

"No," he clarified, "he wants *all of us* to go to dinner. He's going to bring his fiancée, Tori, and I am to bring you."

Rose stiffened in the seat beside him. "Does he… *know?*"

"About Joey? No." Unless Heath had opened his big mouth. "But he knows I've been seeing you. And Tori wants to see you, too. She's missed you since their house was completed and she has no excuse not to cook."

She relaxed a little and chuckled softly. "She ate in the diner nearly every day while she was living in the Airstream. I miss talking to her, too."

"Shall I tell him that Wednesday night works?"

"Sure," she agreed.

Xander slowed to turn off to her apartment and parked at her building. Rotating in his seat, he reached out to cup her cheek and draw her close to him. She leaned in, their lips meeting and sending a shot of need down his spine. Her tongue glided along his as his fingers caressed the soft strands of her dark hair.

Reluctantly he pulled away, eyeing his watch. "When do you have to go to work?" he asked. Perhaps there was time to—

"No," Rose said, answering his unasked question. "But…" she grasped the straps of her tank top and pulled them down her arms until she exposed the edges of the red lace bra she was wearing beneath it "…a little anticipation won't hurt you. You can spend the day fantasizing about taking this off." Her fingertip grazed over the curve of her breast seductively. "See you tonight," she said, adjusting her top and slipping out of the Lexus.

* * *

Rose sipped her wine nervously and chastised herself for it. This dinner should be no big deal. The restaurant was nice, but not so fancy it would intimidate her. The company was pleasant. She'd spent many nights chatting with Wade's fiancée, Tori, at the diner. They'd talked about Tori's romantic ups and downs while she navigated the waters of her relationship with the eldest Eden boy. At first the two had been adversaries, battling over land. One day Tori came into the diner fuming and the next time Rose saw her, she was smitten.

Admittedly, Wade was charming when he wanted to be and handsome, as all the Eden boys were. She remembered the upper classman from the high school campus and the trips she'd made out to the farm. Her older sister had had a huge crush on Wade.

But then and now, she'd only had eyes for Xander.

She turned to look at him. He was wearing a well-tailored suit with a narrow tie. He was talking with Wade, who was just as nicely attired, laughing and cutting up the way brothers did. He seemed very at ease, his political facade put away for the evening.

"How is your son doing, Rose?" Tori asked.

Rose turned her attention to the attractive redhead across the table from her. She'd always thought Tori was a strikingly beautiful woman, with flame-red hair, porcelain skin and ice-blue eyes. Tonight she had on a silk dress that was just the same color as her eyes. It was a stunning combination that made Rose feel decidedly dowdy in the floral sheath dress she'd dug out of the back of her closet.

Tori was a brilliant eco-architect who had designed a stunning home on the hill that overlooked the valley. Beautiful, smart and talented—the trifecta. Fortunately, she wasn't one of those women who realized she was special.

She was very down-to-earth and friendly, even with a small-town nobody like Rose.

"He's great. Getting bigger every day. His broken arm isn't slowing him down at all. He's at scout camp this week."

"Do you have a picture? I haven't seen him in forever."

"Sure." Rose took out her phone and pulled up a recent shot. "Here he is at the parade the other day. Ignore the bright red lips. He'd just eaten a strawberry snow cone."

Tori took the phone and smiled when she saw the picture. "He's grown so much. Turning into quite the little man." As she studied the picture, a curious expression came to her face. Her blue eyes narrowed at the phone and then quickly shot over to Xander and back to the screen. "He's very handsome," she said, her tone pointed as she handed Rose the cell phone back.

Rose felt her heart start to speed up in her chest. Tori knew. One glance and she knew. Her eyes grew wide, words escaping her. What should she say? Xander hadn't wanted to go public yet. He hadn't even told his own family.

"You shouldn't have let his daddy out of your sight," Tori said with a knowing wink. "Oh, I heard about your win at the festival."

Rose finally let the air escape from her lungs and nodded, thankful for the change in subject. Tori wasn't interested in spreading around gossip. She'd probably made a point of letting Rose know she'd figured it out only in case she needed someone to talk to. It would certainly be nice to have someone she could confide in about all this.

"Thanks," she said, a touch of embarrassed color coming to her cheeks. "It's not a very difficult recipe, really."

"Have you had that cake at the diner?" Xander injected himself back into their conversation.

"No," Tori admitted. "I don't think I've ever seen it on the menu. I'd love to try it, though. It sounded divine."

"It's a new item," Rose explained. "I've only made it this summer once the berries came into season. I'm sure since it won, we'll have it on the menu for a while. You two should stop in and have a slice."

"The name strawberry cloud doesn't do it justice. It's like…" Xander's voice trailed off. "I can't even describe it. It's so light and flavorful."

"Like a strawberry cloud?" Wade suggested.

"Yes," Xander replied sarcastically. "Thanks so much."

"We should come by," Tori agreed. "We've been so busy lately. Wedding planning isn't for sissies. And Wade's wrapping up a development project. Seems to be taking up all our time. We've barely seen Xander and he's been in town for two weeks!"

"That's not entirely our fault," Wade pointed out. "I went by the farm twice but Xander was preoccupied." He turned and fixed his dark green gaze on Rose. "I don't know who could be taking up all his time."

"What can I say?" Rose said with a smile and a shrug.

Wade glared at his brother. "It's like you're back in high school again. I recognize the signs."

"Signs?" Xander frowned.

"Oh yeah. I remember when you two started dating. All of a sudden, Xander was distracted and spending all his time doing his hair or trying to bribe us to take on his chores so he could spend more time with Rose."

"Xander was a party to bribery?" Tori said, her mouth open in mock shock.

"Shh!" Xander said, his eyes wide with panic. "Don't say that so loud. If someone heard that, they might not get the joke."

Everyone laughed. "Xander was all about school and

baseball until Rose came around. It's probably a good thing you guys broke it off before he went to Georgetown. He would've flunked out hard."

"Hey," Xander argued, "I managed to date in college without dropping below a three-point-eight grade point average, thank you."

"Yeah. But those were just anonymous college girls. That's not the same as dating Rose. You had him wrapped around your finger," Wade turned to her and said with a smile. "Putty in your hands. And from the looks of it, you've worked your magic on him again."

Rose's eyebrows shot up. She turned to look at Xander, trying to see what Wade saw, but it was the same face that had looked at her the past few weeks. Wade couldn't possibly be right. They were just having fun for old times' sake, right? At least he was. Rose had known she was in too deep the moment she laid eyes on him, but she had held back, knowing it would never be a two-way street.

Or could it?

"It's true," Xander said matter-of-factly, making her heart stutter in her chest for a moment. "She is a tasty treat and I can't get enough." A smile broke out across his face as he turned to Rose and lifted the back of her hand to his lips. His hazel eyes were fixed on her as his warm skin met hers and sent a tingle of awareness through her whole body. "Rose has entranced me with her...*strawberry cloud.*"

"Ugh," Tori said, wrinkling her nose. "You make that sound dirty."

Xander laughed and placed Rose's hand back in her lap. She drew it under the table and smiled to hide her own disappointment. She'd thought for a moment that maybe he was being serious, but that was because she'd forgotten how much the Eden boys all joked around when they were together. Even Brody, the most serious of them all, would have a good laugh with his brothers.

The waiter brought their entrées to the table. Everyone took a few moments to settle into their meals, tasting and seasoning and softly groaning with approval. It was a very good restaurant. Rose had picked a blackened fillet of tilapia that had just the right amount of heat to complement the buttery white meat. With rice and grilled asparagus, as well, she could easily stuff herself.

"What will do you without her strawberry cloud when Congress is back in session?" Wade asked after swallowing a large bite of steak.

At that, Xander frowned at his rib eye. "I don't know," he said, turning to look back at Rose with all signs of humor gone from his face. "We still need to talk about that. There are a lot of unknowns right now."

"Why don't you sweep her off her feet and take her far away from this dull little town?" Tori asked.

"We've hardly b—" Rose started to argue away the importance of their relationship, but she was interrupted by Xander.

"I've given it some serious thought, if she's interested." He turned toward her. "Rose, would you ever consider moving to D.C.?"

"Move to D.C.?" she parroted back to him. Was he asking her to move in with him? With his brother and future sister-in-law as witnesses? Rose certainly couldn't afford to live there on her own. "What would I do there?"

"Whatever you like. You're an award-winning baker. You could try working at one of the nearby bakeries. There's some great ones. You could even open your own."

Open her own bakery? How could he know what she'd dreamed of doing when she couldn't even voice it aloud to another living soul? He knew her better than she believed.

She'd fantasized about opening a bakery, but it required up-front cash that she'd tried, and failed, to save. Every time she'd get a good amount put away, disaster would strike and she'd need new tires or X-rays.

"Yeah. There's some nice bakeries around," he continued, "but nothing like what I've tasted of yours. I think you and Joey would really love D.C. The museums are great and the food is fantastic. No offense, but Daisy's has got nothing on the places around town. Everything from Ethiopian food to Korean barbecue within a few blocks' walk. There are some great private schools in the area, too. We could get tickets to the Washington Nationals games. I think Joey would…"

Xander continued talking, but Rose's disappointment made it hard for her to follow along. She forced a smile on her face and nodded appropriately as he chatted on. She should've known better than to make that mental leap. Really, they'd reunited less than two weeks ago and had had a couple great nights together. That wasn't grounds for anything other than maybe a call for another date. Moving in together so soon? That was a fantasy. He might want her to move to D.C., but it was more about seeing his son than anything else. She was a means to an end.

"I think you lost her at Korean barbecue," Tori said, catching Rose's attention. "I said sweep her off her feet and you're rattling off neighborhood details like a real estate agent."

Rose laughed it off and shrugged away her concern. "I'm not a very adventurous eater. It sounds nice, but maybe we could start with a long weekend visit before we start packing my things."

"Now that you mention it," Xander said, "I do have to go back to D.C. this weekend. The Fostering Families Center is having their annual fund-raising event. It's a very swanky black-tie party. I'm also doing my first signing there to cross-promote the book and the charity. You should come with me."

"Be serious," she said with a nervous laugh. Even if she could take the time off work, and she couldn't, she'd stand out like a sore thumb at a black-tie gala. Her nicest dress had cost her fifty dollars at a department store in Hartford. It probably wouldn't suit the event any more than her awkward shuffle around the dance floor and desperate clinging to Xander.

"I am being serious. I want you to come with me."

"I have to work."

"I don't know, Rose," Wade said. "You know when he wants to, he can be very persuasive. He'll turn that charming politician shtick on your boss and you'll be on a plane to D.C. before you know it."

She appreciated that Wade would think Xander wanted her in D.C. that badly, but she was tougher to convince. If Wade had known the truth, he'd have realized Xander wanted Joey closer. She had no reason to believe that their sexual holiday was something serious. Taking her to D.C. for a romantic weekend was just a way to grease the wheels and convince her she'd enjoy living there.

"That sounds nice and all, but it's a pointless effort. Once you get back to work, you're going to forget all about little old me," she said. "There's a country to be managed, and frankly, you all need to focus on that instead of me. It's not going so well."

"I take my constituents' concerns very seriously," Xander said in his formal politician's voice, and then he propped his arm on the back of her chair and leaned in close to her.

The movement brought a warm rush of his cologne to her nose, reminding her of the night before, when she'd buried her face in his shoulder and shouted the roof down. His light golden eyes were penetrating, his voice no more than a low rumble only she could hear.

"But I've told you before…there is no way, no how, I'd ever forget about you, Rose."

Nine

"I hope that wasn't too painful," Xander said as they got out of his SUV at her apartment.

Rose took out her keys and paused on the sidewalk. "Why would it be painful? I like your brother and his fiancée."

"I know." He followed her up the walkway to her place and they went inside together. "The conversation dipped into some places that seemed to make you uncomfortable. Like you moving to D.C. I could tell you didn't care for that idea. If I had the kind of job where I could move back here, I would, but I—"

"No," Rose interrupted. "It's not that I don't want to move. It's not like we have a lot going on here. Moving there would be the only way for you to spend quality time with your son. That makes sense. It was just difficult having that conversation without being able to mention that *our* son was a key element of us moving down there. And why I'd be able to afford it. And why we seemed to be moving so fast when we've only had a few dates. Your brother seems to think you're in love when that's hardly the case."

Xander snorted. Since when was she the expert on his emotions? Frankly, he didn't know how he felt. He wanted Rose. He didn't want to leave for D.C. and face a lonely bed without her. Was he in love with her? He didn't think so. He had feelings for her, but he couldn't know how much of it was genuine and how much of it was the situation and their past together. Loving her would make their situation easier. They could get married, have a real family together. He liked the idea of that. He just wasn't sure how it would work in practice with his long hours and brutal pace.

What he *did* know was that he didn't care for how easily she dismissed their relationship. "How do you know how I feel, Rose?"

She set her purse down on the coffee table and shook her head. "I don't know, Xander. We've talked about our life with Joey and spending this week together and now maybe moving to D.C...but I'm just not sure where the two of us are going with this."

Xander reached out and gently cupped her cheek. He focused on her dark eyes, which overflowed with doubt. "We don't have to know all the answers right away. There's no rush. I asked you out on a date because I wanted to see you again. I've regretted losing you since the moment you walked away. I just didn't know what to do about it. When I saw you standing there at the diner, I couldn't help myself. I wanted to see if the magic was still there."

"Is it?"

Xander stepped closer until their bodies were nearly touching and wrapped his arms around her waist. He tugged her tight against him, pressing the firm heat of his desire into her stomach. "Oh yeah."

A soft smile curled her lips as she reached up and laced

her fingers together at the base of his neck. She deliberately pressed forward, grinding against his sensitive parts until he had to close his eyes and swear softly. Xander had had Rose the past two nights. Multiple times. But it didn't matter. He'd thought his enthusiasm for her years ago had had more to do with teenage hormones than anything else, but he couldn't blame that now. He had to face the truth.

Rose was the most precious creature he'd ever held in his arms and his body craved her touch. The more he had of her, the more he wanted. A part of him wished he weren't so responsible. Then maybe he could throw caution to the wind and let himself fall hopelessly in love with this woman. The other part of him urged him to hold back. Something would go wrong, and when it did, they wouldn't have the luxury of just walking away from one another again. They had a son to consider.

But he knew, deep down, that he couldn't walk away from Rose again. The first time had been a tragic mistake, however necessary it had seemed then. This time he wasn't sure he had the strength to leave while she still wanted him to stay. Somehow, some way, he would find a way to keep her in his arms where she belonged.

"Joey is important, but this isn't all about him. I asked you out before I knew about him. I kissed you in the parking lot before I knew about him. These last two weeks haven't just been about our son. They've been about us, too. I want to see where this can go, Rose."

"So do I," she admitted softly. "But I don't want to be your dirty little secret, either. I don't want to be a skeleton in your closet that can ruin your reelection campaign."

"You're not," he said. "And I don't want to keep you a secret. Or Joey. I've been thinking about this a lot since that night at the carnival. You were right. I hadn't really thought all this through. I know we agreed to wait to go public, but I think it's unfair to you *and* to me. So I called my lawyer this morning."

"Your lawyer? Why?"

"He's from D.C., so I need him to study up on Connecticut family law and find out what we need to do going forward. I want to legally acknowledge Joey as my son. Then I want to publically disclose his existence and beat the press to the punch. It will just be a happy reunion story with no sharp edge to cut us."

"What about my father?"

If Xander were standing in front of Billy Pierce right now, he'd punch him in the jaw. Somehow he managed to continue ruining things and making Rose worry incessantly without even being around. "You're not your father. If the press brings it up, we'll address it, but I've decided it doesn't have anything to do with you and me and Joey. I think a lot of people have one of *those* relatives."

She nodded blankly, but he could tell she wasn't entirely sold on the idea. "So we go public," she clarified, "and then the whole town knows that I lied to them about Joey."

Xander tried not to laugh at her worries. He couldn't believe there was someone more concerned with appearances than he was. "Why should they care? He's not their son."

"You know how small towns are, Xander. You're going to head back to D.C. and I'll have to face the backlash alone. Half the town already feels sorry for me and the other half ignores me. I don't want to be the center of gossip, or worse, for Joey to be."

"Then I think we need to seriously consider you moving to D.C. You can get away from all of that and start fresh in a big new city that doesn't care about your past."

Her dark eyes widened, her teeth pulling gently at her full bottom lip with concern. "That's one way to avoid

Cornwall gossip, but it's a pretty drastic step. I don't know that we're ready for the kind of commitment."

"We don't have to be. Sharing a child doesn't mean we have to change our relationship trajectory or move faster than either of us is comfortable. If you move to D.C. and we don't work out as a couple, it won't change anything with our arrangement with Joey. But I would hate for us to not give this a chance because we're afraid of something that might not even happen."

She shook her head, diverting her eyes from his. Xander took advantage of her movement to dip down and place a kiss against the long column of her neck. She gasped softly into his ear and leaned farther to give him the access he needed. His lips moved over her soft, pale flesh, tasting the saltiness of her skin and the sharp acidity of the perfume she'd dabbed along her pulse points.

"Come back with me this weekend." He spoke against the column on her throat. "What can it hurt? It might even help."

"How could it help?"

"It might help you figure out what you want. Where the two of us are in this relationship."

His mouth moved up her neck to her earlobe, biting gently and teasing the sensitive spot just behind it. His fingertips stroked her rib cage through the silky fabric of her dress, moving higher until one firm breast filled his hand. His thumb grazed over the hardened tip as it pressed insistently at the fabric, begging for freedom and the pleasure of his touch.

"You want to know where I think we stand, Rose?" Xander asked as he pulled the zipper of her dress down a few inches. It allowed him to tug the straps of her dress down her shoulders to expose the thin satin bra beneath it. His mouth moved over the fabric, dampening it and making her squirm against him. He pulled down the strap and exposed her perfect, full breast.

"Yes," she panted, although he was fairly certain it had nothing to do with the question he asked and everything to do with his hands.

Xander dipped his head and took the firm pink nipple into his mouth. He teased it with his tongue before drawing hard on it and eliciting a sharp gasp from her throat. He tortured her with pleasure for a few more moments before standing upright and focusing his gaze into the dark eyes that were hazy with her desire for him.

"If I have anything to say about it, Rose…my vote is for *very* close together. Come with me this weekend. Please."

"All right," Rose finally agreed with an exasperated smile. "If I can get the time off, I will go. But—" She started to speak but was silenced by Xander's hungry lips on her own.

"No buts," he said, backing her down the hallway to her bedroom.

"This is my place," Xander said, leading Rose through the entryway of his town house and into the living room. "It was built in 1909 but was fully renovated in 1990. I had the hardwood floors refinished and put in some new appliances, but that was about it. The previous owner had taken great care of it." He set down her bags and turned to look at her when she didn't respond.

She was lost in her thoughts, taking in every detail. Rose brushed past him to look up the staircase and step into the large kitchen. It had oak cabinets the same shade as the floors and brown-and-black-swirled granite countertops.

She paused at the kitchen island with the bar-height stools that lined it. He could just picture her serving Joey Pop-Tarts at that counter, a thought that made him smile.

He wasn't certain if he could get Rose to agree to live with him here, but this trip was a start. He needed to convince her that D.C. wasn't scary.

Xander wasn't entirely certain he was succeeding. Rose looked a little overwhelmed. He could tell her brain was struggling to keep up with the fast-paced changes her life had taken since Wednesday night. Once she'd agreed to go with him, the wheels had been set into motion and there'd been no changing her mind.

Sweet-talking her boss into giving her the weekend off was like child's play. Earlier today they drove to Hartford and caught a small charter jet provided by his publisher. The flight was short, but their time in the air was luxurious, with plush leather seats and a flight attendant who plied them with champagne and an amuse-bouche the moment they boarded.

They were picked up by a limousine, which made the rush-hour D.C. traffic a little easier to bear. Fortunately, it wasn't a long drive from Reagan Airport to his town house. He asked the driver to take the scenic route, allowing Rose to see the glowing sights of the National Mall in the dim evening light. He wished he had time to walk with her down to the Reflecting Pool and chat with Lincoln, but if all went well, they would have plenty of opportunity to do that later.

"Do you like it?" he asked.

Rose chuckled and ran her fingers along the exposed brick wall. "It's wonderful." She pushed aside the drapes to look into the small private courtyard in back. "That's the perfect space for entertaining. And this kitchen is like a dream. I love the double ovens and the grill built into the range. I bet you could make—" She paused and turned to him with a smile. "You don't make anything in here, do you?"

"Not at all. I think I've microwaved popcorn and soup."

Rose shook her head and strolled back to the island to lean against the countertop. "Such a waste! And I cook at home in an oven older than Joey. It's really amazing how much space you have. It looks so small from the outside."

"It really is deceiving. It has a full finished basement downstairs that's perfect for a family room. There's three bedrooms upstairs, too."

"It's a big place for just you. How long have you owned it?"

"I bought it a few weeks after I was elected. I decided this was where I belonged and I fell in love with this place the moment I saw the bay window out front. I knew that if and when I married, it would be perfect for a family."

Xander wasn't going to admit to her that the house had felt very empty since he'd moved in. He had envisioned the potential, but as the years went by and he remained single, the town house had almost started to mock him with its large hollow rooms. Just another reason to stay late at work.

But now he could just picture Rose baking in the kitchen while Joey played video games in the basement family room. It was as crystal clear a vision as if she were really there, surrounded by pans and bowls of batter.

"Would you like to see the upstairs?"

Rose nodded, stifling a yawn. "I'd love to get up close and personal with a bed."

Xander smiled and scooped up her bag from the living room. "I can arrange that. We've got a big day tomorrow. You need your rest."

"Big day?" Rose asked, following him up the stairs. "I thought there was just the signing and the party."

"Well, yes. But preparing for those things takes time. I wanted to take you shopping in the morning before the signing. And after, I thought you'd appreciate some salon pampering."

Rose stopped on the stairs and frowned. "You don't think what I packed is nice enough, do you? It's the fanciest thing I had. I don't go to many charity galas."

Xander turned and went back down a few steps until he could tip up Rose's chin and force her to look at him. "Did I say what you brought wasn't good enough?"

"No," she muttered.

"I want to treat you to a day of girlish pleasures. I don't want you feeling self-conscious—like right now—when you walk into that ballroom. I want you to feel beautiful and confident, as if you belong there, because you do. You could walk in the room wearing cutoffs and I'd still think you were the most gorgeous thing I'd ever seen. But I thought you'd prefer something a little more glamorous."

Rose nodded and started back up the stairs beside him. "I didn't want to come up here and be a burden. You have things to do, too. You don't need to spend all your time cleaning me up to take me out."

They reached the landing and he gestured her to go right into the master suite. "Rose, I'm a man. I shower, put on a suit and show up. That's all I'll do ahead of the signing. My publisher sets it all up. I only have to arrive and sign books. I'll switch into a tuxedo before the gala, but again, not a big deal. I'd much rather watch you thoroughly enjoy getting the royal treatment."

He pushed open the French doors that guarded the entrance to his bedroom and stepped aside to let Rose go in ahead of him.

"I feel like I'm already getting the royal treatment. Fancy jets, limousines, champagne…and then this place. My bedroom looks like a cheap hotel compared to yours."

He watched Rose stroll into the only room in the house that felt fully lived-in to him. His bedroom was his retreat, his only perfectly private and safe place in the world. He might have let his decorator go a little overboard in this room, but he loved the result.

"Look at this bed!" she said, gesturing toward the king-size mattress with the massive carved wooden four-poster bedframe that dominated the far wall. The sheets were dark brown silk, like the color of Rose's eyes. The comforter was a delicately stitched patchwork of silk, leather, tapestry and velvet in shades of brown, beige and blue. A large mahogany credenza at the foot of the bed hid away a fifty-inch flat-screen television that would rise up with the push of a button.

"It's just a bed. It might be fancy, but in the end, it serves the same purpose. I recall your bed being most excellent for lovemaking and sleep. What does it matter when my eyes are closed?"

Rose sat down on the edge of the bed and groaned aloud. "It matters. It sure as hell does." She flopped back against it and sighed. "This is like sleeping on a cloud of velvet. Even with my eyes closed, I can tell this is better."

Xander set her bags over near the small seating area and made his way over to where she was lying. "I don't know," he said. He eased onto the bed beside her and propped his head up on his elbow. "I think I need a thorough comparison before I can make a judgment. We should do everything on this bed just the same as we did on yours."

Rose chuckled and turned her head to look up at him. "I thought I needed my rest for the big day ahead."

Xander placed his hand on Rose's stomach and stroked over her blouse to play at the edge of the underwire in her bra. "Sleep is overrated."

Ten

Rose felt like an impostor.

She certainly didn't look like one, thanks to a luxurious private shopping spree at Neiman Marcus and half a day at an upscale salon having her hair, makeup and nails done. She supposed if you threw enough money at the cause, you could transform anyone's appearance. Tonight she looked more like a princess than a waitress.

Her strapless gown was like something out of a fairy tale. It was a shimmering dusky gold, almost pinkish, with intricate beading on the fitted bodice that exploded out into layers of flowing, glittering tulle. It had movement and sparkle, ideal for dancing, and it went perfectly with the strappy gold heels with Swarovski crystals her shopping assistant had chosen.

Her hair was swept up into an elegant twist that highlighted the long line of her neck and décolletage. She wore a rose-gold choker studded with tiny diamonds at her throat

and a matching bracelet on her wrist. She looked sophisti-
cated and elegant—as though she fit in with the rich and
important people all around her.

But that was on the outside. On the inside she was just
a nobody from Cornwall. A single mother. A waitress.
The daughter of a felon. Surely there wasn't enough fancy
clothing and makeup to cover that up. Eventually, someone would notice she didn't belong here.

Walking into the ballroom on Xander's arm, she'd felt
like Cinderella going to the ball, minus the mice and the
pumpkins. Her fairy godmother came in the form of a
black American Express card with Xander's name on it.
Her prince had bought her entire outfit for tonight, plus
a more casual dress she'd worn to his afternoon signing.
Rose couldn't look at the total when they were done, but
he hadn't even flinched, signing the slip with a smile.

Now he beamed with pride beside her. He'd wanted
Rose to be confident and he'd given her every reason to
feel as if she fit in. Every eye that fell on her was followed
with a warm smile in greeting. Some of the men's gazes
were heated with attraction. Some of the women's eyes
were tainted with a touch of jealousy. But they all looked
at her. Or at least, they looked at Xander and then wondered who the woman with him was.

"Are you okay?" Xander asked as they blended into
the crowd.

Rose nodded, but it was a lie. She didn't want him to
know how nervous she was when he was so concerned about
her enjoying herself tonight. She appreciated how hard he
was trying to make this trip special. He genuinely wanted
her to move to the area. She should be happy that he wanted
to spend as much time with Joey as he could. That he was
willing to support them in a town so expensive.

Instead she was waiting for the other shoe to drop. It always did.

"Would you like some champagne?" Xander asked. There were several bars set up along the edges of the ballroom and one nearby.

"Please," she said, although she knew that meant being left alone for a few minutes. It was worth it to get enough of a buzz to relax her body and mind. Maybe then she could enjoy herself the way he wanted her to.

Xander squeezed her hand and then disappeared through the crowd of people to the bar.

Rose took a deep breath once she was alone to calm herself. There really wasn't a threat she could see. Just a bunch of rich people mingling and sipping cocktails. Not exactly a dangerous situation, but still her heart was racing, her body tense and prepared for a fight-or-flight response.

Her entire life, she'd doubted that she would ever be able to make it in Xander's fast-paced, glamorous world. When Xander had asked her to come with him to Georgetown, she'd been too afraid to go. Even if her mother hadn't been sick, she would've sought out an excuse. Fate had forced her hand and here she was in D.C., testing the waters at last. She was certain that she would immediately be fingered as an outsider, but so far, so good. She'd gotten a few glances, but at least no one had called security on her.

At his book signing this afternoon, she'd sat beside him the whole time. She'd made herself useful by opening up the books to the correct page for him to autograph. There must have been at least two hundred people in line to see him, many with touching stories about their own foster experiences. Xander had been gracious to them all, making each person who came up feel important, even after three solid hours. He had an amazing way with people.

She had to admit that the clothes and the salon treatment were nice, but they weren't what gave her the confidence to come to this party. They weren't what encouraged her to stand taller and smile at strangers. It was Xander's faith in her. He sincerely believed in her. He didn't see the other people here as being better than she was. Xander inspired her to be the best version of herself she could be. She wanted to be the kind of woman Xander could love someday.

She glanced over her shoulder at the line for the bar. He was standing there, chatting with the woman ahead of him. His Valentino tuxedo fit him like a second skin, his black satin bow tie the perfect touch to his flawlessly starched white shirt. He looked so handsome with his light brown hair brushed back and his wide, charming smile. The elegant-looking woman talking to him seemed dazzled. She leaned in, placing a light hand on his lapel as she laughed at something Xander said.

Rose sighed and turned away. She didn't want to watch anymore. She didn't know anything about that woman, but it only took a moment for her to know in her heart that this woman was more suitable for Xander than she would ever be.

"Here you go. One glass of courage."

Startled, Rose spun on her heels to find Xander standing behind her with champagne flutes in each hand. "Thank you," she said, taking the one he offered. She took a healthy sip, closing her eyes and feeling the warmth spread from her stomach to the rest of her body. It did wonders to calm her. After a moment, she was finally able to focus on the party itself and not on that woman or whether or not everyone was looking at her. "So what is the schedule for tonight?"

Xander picked up a program from one of the nearby tables. "Looks like mingling, dinner, speeches and then dancing. Somewhere in there they'll plug my book and ask for money. I'm sure they'll be a lot more subtle, though."

"Sounds like we have a long night ahead." She eyed her mostly empty glass. "I'm going to need more champagne."

"Not necessarily. We can leave now, if you like."

Rose frowned and turned to him. She hadn't expected that at all. Why buy all these fancy clothes just to leave after ten minutes? "Why?" she asked. "Did I do something wrong?"

Xander slipped his arm around her waist and pressed his palm against her hip to pull her closer. "Not at all. I just underestimated how beautiful you were going to look tonight. You always look amazing, but with the hair and the dress, it's enough to make a man weak in the knees. It's like prom all over again. I can't wait to get you home and out of that gown."

She glanced down at the beaded sweetheart neckline of her dress and the ample cleavage on display. It was more than she was normally comfortable showing, but she couldn't help it. The moment she'd stepped into this gown at the store, she'd known it was the one. Xander had told her not to look at the price tags, so she hadn't. She'd just tried to pick the dress that made her feel the prettiest. Any doubts she'd had were erased the moment she stepped out of the dressing room and met Xander's approving gaze.

He liked it as much as she did. She hadn't even bothered trying on any more dresses. It was *the* dress. So she didn't exactly feel like casting it to the ground in a fevered rush. "I hate to disappoint you, but even if we go home right now, I'm not taking this dress off. It's too beautiful and I look too good in it. I might even sleep in it."

Xander rubbed a bit of the rough golden tulle between his fingertips and shook his head. "I don't recommend that. But if you want to leave it on, I can always just flip all this fabric up over your head."

Rose laughed and slapped his hand away as he tugged at the layers of her skirt. She would never understand how he could be in a room of such beautiful and powerful women and only have eyes for her. "We're not going home. You promised me a party with dancing and we're sticking it out."

Xander opened his mouth to argue with her but was interrupted when a woman came onto the stage and asked everyone to take their seats. Defeated, he escorted her to a table near the front and helped her into her chair. They sat through several courses and several speeches. Most of the speakers praised Xander for his contributions to Fostering Families, including donating a portion of his book sales to the organization. The cover was projected onto a screen and attendees were reminded that Xander had autographed copies in advance that were available for purchase during the event.

After they spoke, the servers brought out the dessert course. Hers was what they called a chocolate bomb. It had a layer of hardened dark chocolate over a decadent dome of light chocolate mousse. It had a dense brownie crust and a toasted hazelnut in the very center. She dissected the dessert as she ate it, trying to figure out exactly how she could re-create it for the diner.

By the time she'd figured it out, Rose realized that she'd lost Xander. From the moment they stepped out of their car at the hotel, he'd had people talking to him. It had stopped during the meal and speeches, but now attendees were up dancing and mingling again. Xander was a few feet away chatting with a couple gentlemen she didn't know. It looked as though he'd gotten one bite of his dessert before he was hijacked.

That was a shame. It was good.

Rose tried entertaining herself, waiting for him to return. She finished her dessert and chatted idly with the woman beside her. The woman's husband had also vanished. Looking around the room, there were more than a few ladies sitting at their tables talking while men clustered in groups. Rose finally excused herself to get another drink and milled around the ballroom. The edges of the room were decorated with photos and other displays from the Fostering Families Center over the years.

At last she made a circle back to her table. Her drink was empty and the balls of her feet were aching. It had been a long night and it was time for this coach to become a pumpkin again. Xander had been missing for almost an hour. Why had he even brought her to this event? He could've come alone and not felt guilty about ignoring his date half the night. If he didn't show up soon, she was going to get a cab. She'd just have to figure out where he lived first....

"Would you honor me with a dance, Miss Pierce?"

Rose turned in her seat to find Xander the Elusive had returned to her side. "I'd about given up on you."

"I know. I'm sorry. I've broken free. Dance with me before someone else comes up."

She reluctantly got up and let Xander lead her to the dance floor. Despite the late hour, it was still crowded with couples dressed in their finest.

"You're so stiff," Xander complained. "Relax. Dancing is supposed to be fun."

Rose shook her head. "I'm not sure why you brought me with you to this. I should've just stayed in Connecticut where I belong."

Xander stilled on the dance floor, his brow furrowed

with concern. "Why would you say that? Aren't you having a good time?"

"I am," she sighed. "It's fine, but you're busy. Everyone
wants to talk to you. I feel like I'm a burden."

"You're anything but a burden. In fact, you're the only
one here that *I* want to talk to. No matter what you think
or how much you worry, know this—I want you here. You
belong here. With me. Not just tonight, but every night."

Rose gasped, the sound swallowed by the big-band
music. Xander pressed his palm into the small of her back
and began moving again, pulling her across the floor with
him. She could only cling to him and follow his lead.

When the song ended, they stayed on the dance floor,
Xander holding her close and looking deep into her eyes.
"I don't just want you to move to D.C., Rose. I want you to
move in with me. I want us to be a family. A real family."

Rose couldn't breathe and it had nothing to do with
the dancing. It was wonderful. Amazing. Fantastic. But it
was Xander's words that had truly thrown her for a loop.

He wanted her to move to D.C. and live with him. That
meant he really was serious about going public with their
relationship and with Joey's paternity. He didn't care about
her father's criminal past. She was just blown away. And
a part of her was thrilled and relieved.

The other part of her was scared to death he was making a huge mistake. Would it really be the nonevent he
believed it all to be? Was it possible that they could have
the happily-ever-after she'd fantasized about? She tried to
look at the bright side, but life had taught her that things
didn't always work out the way you planned.

She pushed those thoughts out of her mind and instead
grasped at his tuxedo lapels with both hands. With a hard
tug, she brought his mouth down to hers. She poured all

of her anxiety, all of her fears, all of her excitement and anticipation into the kiss. He met her measure for measure, wrapping his arms around her waist and pressing her tight against him.

"Take me home," she said at last when their lips parted. *Home,* she thought. Could that beautiful town house really be her home someday?

Xander took her hand and led her through the crowd to the exit. They waited anxiously for their car to pull up out front and then rushed into the house the moment they arrived. Rose kicked off her painful shoes in the entryway, then ran barefoot up the stairs with Xander on her heels.

They burst into his bedroom together, the chase turning into a slower pursuit as Rose turned to face him. He slowly backed her across the floor until she felt her spine meet with the carved wood post of the bed.

When she stopped, Xander slipped out of his jacket and tugged off his tie. Then he knelt down. "I'm going in," he said with a sly smile as he sought out the hem of her dress and tugged it up high enough to disappear under its layers. She felt his fingers gently stroking her upper thighs, his hot breath searing her bare skin. She braced her hands on the wooden column behind her when his fingertips grazed across the satin of her panties. She stiffened as he applied pressure to just the right spot and a bolt of pleasure shot through her.

"Oh, Z," she whispered, her eyes fluttering closed. She felt his hands seek out the waist of her panties and gently start tugging them down the length of her legs. Rose adjusted her stance, kicking out of them and leaving herself completely bare beneath the exquisite gown.

Xander let his hands roam all over the soft skin of her legs, creeping higher and higher. She felt the flutter of his touch running along the cropped curls of her sex, then the explosion of sensation as one finger dipped deeper and stroked her aching, moist core. Her heart started racing in her chest as he pushed her closer and closer to her release.

Her orgasm was hard and intense, very nearly rocking her off her feet with the powerful spasms. Only his steady grip on her waist kept her stable until the last tremors shook her legs.

Xander climbed out from under her gown and stood to pull her into his arms. She was like a rag doll, stumbling against his hard body. She felt as if there were no more bones left in her legs. "I've got you," he said. "I won't let you fall."

She knew that. Unlike her father, Xander meant it. Even back in school, Rose always knew she could count on Xander to be there for her. When her mother's time was short and her father was only worried about himself, he'd been the constant in her life. She felt as if she could do anything with him beside her.

And when she pushed him out of her life, she'd been in a free fall. When she needed him the most, she'd been too scared to ask for his support. The cost had been too high. But it had taught her to stand on her own. She could survive without him, even if she didn't want to.

Now he seemed to be offering her the opportunity for the two of them to try again. She was tired of being alone. If she was honest with herself, she wanted Xander back. Rose wanted him in her bed and in her life and her son's life. If that meant moving to D.C., she would go.

Rose turned her back, holding the post once again to offer the zipper of her dress to him. She felt the graze of his fingertips at her shoulder blades where the dress began, and then heard the loud slide down to the base of her spine.

Xander put his warm palms on her back, wrapping around her rib cage to open up the bodice and push the dress down. The fabric skimmed down her body and pooled at her feet as if she were standing in a fluffy golden nest. She stepped out of the dress and then turned to face Xander.

He had his hand at his collar, quickly unfastening the buttons of his shirt. He tossed aside his shirt and whipped off his belt. Rose's fingers sought out his fly, undoing the button and pulling the zipper down. Her hand slipped inside, slowly stroking the firm heat of him through his briefs.

"Rose," he groaned, and then his mouth slammed against hers. She met his intensity, stroking him with a sure, firm hand and pushing his slacks out of her way. She was about to slip beneath the waistband of his briefs when he pushed forward and she fell backward onto the bed.

Before she could recover, Xander had slipped from his briefs and was moving above her. The heat of his skin scared hers as he glided over her body. Rose's thighs parted, cradling him. He paused only as he met her eye to eye and hovered there.

He was such a beautiful man. Perfectly made for appearing on television. A face that could inspire trust and lead his fellow congressmen. The angles and curves of his face could change to make him look more serious, handsome, charming or boyishly playful when he smiled and those dimples came out. His sandy hair had fallen into his eyes, the flaming desire flickering there as tiny golden flecks amid the green and brown.

Was it possible that a man like this could ever love a woman like her? He said he wanted to be a family, but she was no one. Plain and hardworking at best, poor criminal trash at worst. She didn't deserve the love of a man like Xander, but she wanted it so badly her heart nearly burst at the thought of it.

Xander dipped his head to kiss her and she closed her eyes to lose herself in the sensation of being with him. She could feel the tears gathering in the corners as the emotions swelled inside her. She had been lying to herself about her feelings. As much as she argued that things were moving too fast, it wasn't for a lack of emotions on her part. It was the worry that her heart was barreling ahead, leaving Xander behind.

She loved him. Rose had tried to put years and excuses between her and her heart to reason away how she felt, but it didn't matter. She had never stopped loving her charming teenage love. Not many people met the love of their life in a sophomore geometry class, but she had. And now he was back in her life and in her bed. This felt like a dream, but it was a reality she'd fantasized about for so long.

His lips parted from hers, the air heavy and warm between them. Her lungs burned from breathing so hard, but it didn't matter. It hurt more to be without him.

He shifted against her, his spine arching and his hips moving forward. He entered her. Slowly. Leisurely. Rose arched her back to take all of him in. It felt like an eternity before he stopped moving and when he did, she could hardly tell where she ended and he began. Xander was in her blood, his scent in her lungs, his taste on her lips.

His light eyes searched her face for a moment as he hovered, buried deep and still inside her. "I've missed you, Rose," he said. "I don't ever want to miss you again."

It wasn't a declaration of love, but it was enough for Rose to let the last of her defenses down. He wanted her in his life, not because of Joey but because he wanted her. It was something she had never dared to hope to hear again in her life.

"You won't," she said. Her fears weren't gone, but in the moment, she felt bold enough to face them. "If you want us to move to D.C., we will."

"Really?" A broad smile crossed his face.

"Yes, really."

Xander kissed her and the moment that had hung suspended in time suddenly began to rush forward. Emboldened by her response, Xander eased back and thrust forward again. And then again.

Rose clung to him, riding the waves of pleasure as they surged through her body. She drew her knees up and locked her ankles together at the small of his back. She didn't want to let him go, not even for a moment. This moment wouldn't last forever, but she would savor it as long as she could.

He buried his face in her neck and drove into her. Every inch of their bodies was touching, their skin heated and slick with sweat. It wasn't long before she felt her release building up in her again. She bit her lip, trying hard to fight it off. It was too soon.

"I'm not ready for this moment to end," she admitted. It was easier to say when she didn't have to look him in the eye. "I want to keep this moment forever."

Xander propped himself up onto his elbows and planted kisses along her jawline to her lips. He kissed her thoroughly and smiled. "There will be more moments. Many more. Enjoy this one."

His hand slid up her outer thigh to her knee. He hooked her leg over his shoulder, tilting her pelvis up and driving harder and deeper than ever before. The sensation was incredible, causing Rose to cry out.

"Oh, Z," she gasped, clawing at his back. There was no use in prolonging her release now. It was impossible. She could feel the tightening in her belly, the driving surge of the explosives getting ready to burst inside her. "Yes, yes!"

"Let go, Rose," he coaxed in a harsh whisper. "Just let go."

It was a hard command to follow. She spent most of her life fighting. But with Xander, she could let go. Let him do some of the fighting for her. She sucked a large lungful of air and her eyes closed. Like a tsunami, her orgasm crashed through her. She clung to Xander for dear life as every nerve ending in her body lit up and her insides pulsated with pleasurable shocks.

"Xander!" she yelled at its peak.

"Rose, Rose…" he repeated in response, driving harder and faster than before until he stiffened and groaned. He gasped her name one last time as he surged into her body, leaving him exhausted and trembling.

He dropped over to her side, sucking ragged breaths into his lungs as his muscular chest rose and fell. They both lay together quietly for a few moments before Rose pushed herself up onto her elbow to look down at him. His hair was damp and plastered to his forehead. His brow was furrowed as he lay with his eyes closed and his hands just barely trembling.

It made her think of the very first time they'd made love. Ken had loaned Xander his truck to take her to dinner and a movie, but they'd opted for a picnic by the river with a blanket spread out in the truck bed. Under a blanket of stars, she'd given herself to him, heart and soul. Afterward she remembered looking at him as he lay just like this. A dozen years had passed since that moment, but it seemed as though she'd never gotten either of them back.

He had her, still. Heart and soul.

Eleven

We have a problem, the text from Brody read. Deborah Wilder just identified the remains of her brother.

Xander's stomach sank. Returning to Cornwall and reality after his fantastic time with Rose in D.C. was hard enough. He wasn't ready to face this yet.

He set his glass of tea on the kitchen counter of Rose's apartment and frowned at his phone. The moment of truth had arrived. And the timing couldn't be worse. There was never a good time for that sort of thing, but they were on the verge of telling Joey that Xander was his father. He needed to be here with Rose and his son for this big moment, not at the farm fighting off the press and police that would come when the news broke. But that was why he was here. Why he'd returned to Cornwall in the first place.

Xander looked up from his phone. Joey was playing a video game on the television, shooting at zombies or something. He was wearing a headset that allowed him to talk to players networked in other places around the world. A far cry from the Nintendo Game Boy he'd had at Joey's age. Fortunately, his son was immersed in slaying the undead and oblivious to everything going on around him.

Rose was in the shower. He could still hear the water running. They'd returned to Cornwall on a morning flight and then driven to camp to pick up Joey that afternoon. Rose wanted to shower and change before they shared the big news with Joey and, assuming all was received well, went out for a celebratory family dinner.

His gaze drifted back to the words on his screen. How? he managed to type despite how badly his shaking fingers were stymying him.

His ring, Brody texted back.

Xander silently cursed and refrained from texting the same sentiment. Of course. He had burned all of Tommy's things that night, but they'd all been too freaked out by the body itself to remove anything from him. Tommy had always worn a large gold ring with a black onyx stone in the middle. It was large, like a class ring, and left a distinctive welt on the skin if it came in contact with your face. Wade had found that out the hard way. Xander had luckily not gotten close enough to Tommy's hands to get a good look at it, but it was distinctive enough for someone, especially his own sister, to recognize. He'd always worn that ring and it had been buried along with Tommy.

After all these years, it was probably the only thing left behind and damned if it wasn't the one thing that someone would recognize.

She heard about the unidentified remains and called Sheriff Duke. He asked her to come down from Hartford and take a look. They're working to match dental records. Expect things to start happening anytime now, Brody added.

Before he could respond, his phone started to ring. It was Heath. Word was spreading fast. He got up from the barstool and carried his phone with him into the bedroom. The water was still running, so he had time to take the call.

"Hey," Xander answered, his tone flat. He sat on the edge of the bed and muted the television that was playing.

"You hear from Brody?" Heath asked, skipping pleasantries.

"Yes."

"Are you at the farm?"

"No," Xander admitted. "I'm at Rose's apartment. We were…going to *tell* Joey tonight."

Heath whistled softly through his teeth. "I'm sorry. Not the best day to ID a body. What are you going to do?"

"Postpone, I guess. Hopefully, she'll understand."

"Xander," Heath began, and then paused. "It's probably all going to come out now. What happened that night. I've been thinking about this awhile and I've decided that I'm okay with it. I know it isn't all about me. You all have something at stake here, too. But I don't want you to do something you'll regret trying to protect me."

"Of course I will. You're—"

"No, Xander. Listen to me."

Heath's voice was firm, resolved and very much unlike him. Xander didn't like it. He much preferred his carefree, fun younger brother. Why fate had trapped a boy so young and innocent into such a terrible deed, he would never know. He'd wished a hundred times that he had been the one to find them. That he had been the one to stop Tommy.

"I'm tired of all of this. I think the game is up. You have your own family to protect now. That's more important than taking care of me. I'm a grown man, now, not a child. It's not ideal, but I will tell my story and deal with the consequences. I don't want this hanging over our heads any longer."

"What about Mom and Dad?"

There was an extended silence on the line. "I'll tell them. I think Dad will understand what I was doing and why we couldn't tell him before now. Hopefully, I can beat the cops to the punch."

"What about Julianne? Have you spoken with her?"

He heard Heath sigh. "No, but I'm certain we're on the same page. She's been under this dark cloud for as long as we have. All of us knew this moment would come eventually. She probably feels responsible for it."

"They'll make her come back and make a statement. You, too."

"I've been thinking about taking a few months off from the firm anyways. Things are going well. I think my partner can take the reins for a while. I need to spend some time in Cornwall and deal with all of this. I can't do it from Madison Avenue."

"So what do you want me to do, Heath? Just let it happen? I can't do that. Don't ask me to. I came to Cornwall to handle this and now you're asking me to forget why I'm even here."

"I'm not saying you should march into the police station and confess everything. But be prepared for it to unravel. I am."

Xander didn't know what to say. He'd spent more than half of his life protecting this secret. It was against his nature to just let the truth come out now.

The water in the bathroom turned off. Rose would come out any minute. "I've got to go," he said. "I need to talk to Rose."

"Good luck with everything," Heath said. "I can't wait to meet my nephew. And for Mom to find out. I really want to be there when she does. I want a front-row seat and popcorn."

As if he didn't already have enough to worry about. "Shut up, man."

He heard his brother laugh, and then the line went dead. Shaking his head, Xander slipped his phone into his pocket and tried to think of what he would say when Rose came out. Like any political speech, he thought through his words and practiced it several times in his head. It made him wish he had one of his staffers here to help him draft something. He never was the best speech writer.

She exited the bathroom a moment later. Her body was still slightly damp and wrapped in a fluffy cotton towel. Her hair was wet and combed out down her back in long straight strands. She smiled at him as she settled onto the bed and started rubbing lotion into her legs.

He was afraid to open his mouth. He, the politician, the master of spin. He, the one who always knew just what to say and when, couldn't find the words. Somehow he just knew that the second he started to speak, things would change. He would never be able to get back to this moment where she smiled at him, so loving and trusting.

Xander wanted this to work with Rose. He wanted them to move to D.C. and start a life with him there. But every bit of that fantasy was riding on her reaction to what he was about to say.

"Rose," he said, "I hate to do this, but I have to take a rain check on tonight."

Her dark eyes narrowed at him as she finished applying her lotion and stood up. "On tonight? I thought we decided it was The Night. That's a pretty big event to skip out on. What's going on that's suddenly more important?"

"I know it's a big deal. I've been looking forward to and dreading this moment since we decided to tell him.

I'm so nervous that he won't like me or that he'll hate me for not being in his life."

Rose moved around the bed to sit shoulder by shoulder next to him. "He's not going to hate you. He adores you. Finding out that you're his father will only make it that much sweeter for him. It's like finding out Superman is your dad."

"There's no superpowers to be inherited," Xander said drily. "Just my chaotic political life."

"Are you wanting to wait because you're nervous about it?" She patted his knee reassuringly. "It's going to be fine, really."

He ran his fingers though his hair. "No. I'd much rather do it and get it done so I can stop being so anxious, but I don't want to do it and rush out. Can we postpone a day or two?"

"Why not," she said with an undertone of sarcasm. "We've already waited ten years. Really, what is more important than this, Xander? Tell me."

"Rose, please." Xander said. "I've got to get back to the farm. There's an emergency I need to take care of."

Her irritation was quickly replaced by concern. "What happened? Are Ken and Molly okay?"

"Yes, they're fine. There's just something going on there that I have to be home for. It's the reason I came to town in the first place."

"Something going on?" she repeated. "Get a little more vague, Xander." Rose turned away from him and looked up at the television silently playing in front of them. The local station had cut into the syndicated television show to broadcast breaking news.

Xander couldn't hear the newscaster, but the image over the woman's shoulder said Body Identified. As usual, Brody's information had been correct and timely. The truth was out.

* * *

Rose picked up the remote and turned the sound of the television back on.

"…remains discovered on the former Garden of Eden property have been identified as that of seventeen-year-old Tommy Wilder. Tommy was a foster child taken in by Ken and Molly Eden, the owners of the Garden of Eden Christmas Tree Farm, several weeks before his disappearance. His sister, Deborah Wilder Curtis of Hartford, identified the body yesterday and dental records have confirmed the match."

"Rose…" Xander said, but she ignored him and turned the sound up another notch on the television.

"Tommy Wilder was reported missing by his foster parents more than fifteen years ago. All of the boy's belongings were missing from his room and a note was found by one of the other foster children indicating that he ran away. Police will be questioning Ken and Molly Eden to try to piece together what happened the night of Tommy's disappearance."

Rose swallowed hard and tried to process the information. She remembered Tommy Wilder. He was a senior when he came to live with Xander's family. The few times Rose came to the farm while he was staying with them, she'd been thoroughly creeped out. She'd been a girl who spent most of her time being ignored, and Tommy's heavy appraisal of her had been unnerving and unwelcome. She'd been admittedly relieved when he ran away. It had gotten to the point where she didn't want to come to the farm or she wouldn't let Xander out of her sight if she did.

After Tommy's disappearance, she and Xander had hit one of the low points in their relationship. They hadn't been dating long, but things changed quickly. He'd suddenly become distant. He had canceled a few of their dates and made excuses not to see her. For a while she'd been certain that he was going to break up with her. Even the other Eden boys had avoided talking to her or anyone else.

Then, after a few weeks, her old Xander came back to her. He had told her that they were all concerned about Tommy running away and all the police attention around the farm. As foster children, they could be placed in a new home at any time if the parents were deemed unfit. The Edens were the fittest parents in the world, but she could understand that it might look bad with Tommy running away.

Things had returned to normal and after that point, she'd forgotten all about Tommy Wilder. Apparently, the story had not ended as neatly as it seemed. Xander had been excited to talk to Joey today. They had a great afternoon planned as a family. Now he was agitated and wanted to bail on the whole thing to go home. This had to be why.

"You call that *something,* Xander?"

He sighed and stood up, shaking his head. "What do you want me to say, Rose? I have to go home and protect my family from scandal and criminal charges?"

Rose lifted the remote to turn off the television and slowly got up from the bed. When she looked at Xander, she saw an expression there that she'd never expected to see. Guilt. His hazel eyes couldn't quite meet hers, the corners of his mouth slightly downturned as if he was trying to think of what to say. His hands were thrust in his pockets and his shoulders were hunched over.

Her father had looked the same way when she visited him the first time in jail after the robbery. They couldn't afford bail, so he was locked up for the months leading to his trial. Long before he was convicted, there'd been guilt in his eyes and his broken stance that he couldn't hide from her.

"Protect your family or protect yourself?" she asked.

"I want to protect *everyone*," he clarified. "Including you and Joey."

"Xander," she said very slowly and deliberately. "Look at me. Do you know what happened to Tommy Wilder?"

His eyes reluctantly met hers and he nodded almost imperceptibly.

"He didn't run away, did he?"

Xander turned his back to her and took a few steps away to examine the collage of pictures on her wall. He studied them in great detail before he spoke.

"You noticed what the news left out of that broadcast, didn't you? That his parents lost custody of him because they couldn't control him? That he was suspended for fighting and bringing a switchblade to school? That he'd been arrested for theft and assault? He was under eighteen, so all that got swept under the rug. Now that he's dead, they've conveniently forgotten he was a rotten person. They talked about him like he was an abused child instead of a two-hundred-pound menace."

He was right, but she was afraid to follow where he was going with that. "So you're saying he deserved it?" she asked hesitantly.

Xander turned on his heel to look at her. She watched his expression shift as he fought with the words he really wanted to say. He probably wanted to say yes, he did deserve it. But he wouldn't. He'd run it through his political filter first. "I'm saying that *whatever* happened to him, they need to consider that he probably brought it on himself."

He wouldn't say the words, but he didn't have to. Whatever happened on the farm all those years ago, Xander had been involved. The hows and whys didn't matter. She was certain her father had reasons for doing what he'd done.

He'd probably stated them in the hundred letters she'd thrown away. In the end, nothing changed the truth and nothing would bring the dead back to life.

"I suppose it's just as well that we don't talk to Joey today. Under the circumstances, perhaps we shouldn't tell him at all."

"Rose, wait. This doesn't change our plans or how I feel about you or Joey. I just need time to work this out."

She detected a pleading edge in his voice. Her father had pleaded with her, but it had fallen on deaf ears just as Xander's pleas did now. She'd thought that loving Xander would be a safe choice—as far away on the spectrum from her father as she could get. Xander was a politician who carefully dodged scandal. He certainly wouldn't commit a crime, right? She felt so foolish. Some people would say that all politicians were criminals to different degrees.

"Time to work it out?" Rose rushed into the bathroom and came out wrapped in her robe. She couldn't have this conversation in a flimsy bath towel. "How long, Xander? Ten to fifteen? He already has a criminal for a grandfather. Do you honestly think I'm going to let him have a criminal for a father, too?"

Xander flinched and his jaw tightened in response. "I'm not a criminal, Rose. You don't understand."

"Of course I don't. I'm just a silly law-abiding citizen trying to live a decent life, and everyone around me seems hell-bent on dragging me down with them. I don't know what happened that night, Xander, and I'm not sure I want to know. It's bad enough that I know how the night ended."

"It's not as simple as that, Rose."

"I don't know what I was thinking," she said, ignoring him as her blood pumped furiously in her ears. "Just like the rest of the voting public, I sat back and ate up all your practiced and polished words, but they didn't mean anything. All this time, all the promises you made about our future together, our future with Joey, you were just talking big. Nothing but lies."

Color suddenly rushed to Xander's face and clenched jaw. "Lies? I meant everything I said to you. If we're going to talk about lies, Rose, how about the ones you've been spouting to the whole town for the last ten years, huh?"

"How dare you even compare those two things! I didn't kill anyone. I just protected your career."

"And made a fine martyr of yourself in the process. Don't throw stones, Rose. Neither of us is innocent."

"Look what telling the truth got me, Xander! How dare you demand to be a part of your son's life knowing full well that you might end up in jail one day!" She shook her head, the tears making her vision blurry. "All this time, you've been sweet-talking me, trying to convince me to come to D.C. and move in with you.... It's too late for me, but I very nearly let you become important to my *son*."

The anger faded from his expression for just a moment. "What do you mean it's too late for you?"

"I mean that I'm a fool. Damn you, Xander Langston, for tricking me into loving you just so I could have my heart broken again."

"Rose, I don't want to br—"

"Get out," she demanded. For the past eleven years, Rose had been reeling from the day she walked out of Xander's life. She'd been afraid to take a deep breath since he'd returned, worried he would disappear. She wasn't about to sit around and wait for him to leave, this time in handcuffs. Just like before, she would take matters into her own hands and walk away before he could leave her.

Xander's jaw dropped. "Wait. Can we talk about this?"

Rose angrily shook her head. "No, we can't. On this

point things are nonnegotiable. I will not have a criminal as my son's father."

"I am not a criminal!" Xander shouted. "And even if I was, I'm still his father. You can't change that."

He was right. The past was the past. "You're right. Everyone makes mistakes. But I can change the future. You and I are done. And until whatever that is—" she gestured toward the television "—is cleared up, I don't want you seeing Joey. You say you're not a criminal? Prove it. Until then, I want you to get out of my apartment."

"Rose—"

"Now!" she nearly shrieked, hopeful that Joey still had his headphones on. They'd managed to keep their anger on a manageable level, but she was at her limit.

Apparently, so was he. Xander nodded and backed away from her toward the door. "It was good seeing you again, Rose." He turned the handle and walked out of the bedroom, picking up his overnight bag as he waved to Joey and slipped out the front door.

With him gone, every bone in Rose's body disintegrated. She flopped down onto the bed, her tears rushing out of her almost faster than her body could make them.

Twelve

Xander blew into his quiet, empty town house much later than he'd planned. The drive back from Connecticut had been fairly uneventful until he hit a bad accident on the interstate. It had left him stranded between exits for several hours as victims were transported by helicopter and cars were towed away. By the time his Lexus pulled up in front of his town house, it was nearly midnight.

The perfect capstone to two miserable weeks. It had started going downhill the minute he returned to Cornwall with Rose. Perhaps coming back to the comfort and safety of the Capitol would swing luck back in his favor.

Starting tomorrow. Tonight he was too exhausted to care about luck. He carried his luggage in and dropped it at the bottom of the stairs. He was too tired to carry it up right now. Eyeing the leather sofa in the sitting room, he seriously considered sleeping on the couch. His bed felt as though it were miles away and he couldn't drag himself another step.

At the same time, he doubted he could sleep even in the comfort of his bed. His weary mind was endlessly spinning. Thoughts of Rose and how badly they'd parted. Leaving Joey behind without being able to tell him what was going on. Tommy's body. Heath's defeated voice on the phone. His parents' worried expressions as they were interrogated again by Sheriff Duke.

The past two weeks had been ones you couldn't pay him to live over, but perhaps the worst was behind him now. By the time he prepared to head home, things seemed to have quieted down on the farm. The cloud of potential problems still hung over their heads as it had for years, but for now, the case had reached a standstill.

Xander stumbled into the kitchen, pulled a bottle of Scotch from the cabinet and poured himself a few fingers' worth over ice. He climbed onto one of the barstools and idly sorted through the stack of mail he'd left sitting there.

The Scotch burned as it went down, splashing into his empty stomach with a roar. The warmth spread through his veins and worked quickly to unknot the tense muscles in his shoulders and neck. He should've made a trip to the Wet Hen while he was there dealing with the cops. He was wound up tighter than a pocket watch and deserved a drink or two after fielding the press and the police at the farm.

That, at least, was easier than watching his parents deal with the tragic news. His cheerful, optimistic mother had been beside herself when she found out that the body belonged to her missing foster child. Molly had never quite forgiven herself for failing Tommy, despite her successes with so many other children. She hadn't so much as raised a finger to Tommy, but she was consumed with misplaced guilt. She couldn't even speak to the police the first day, she was so upset.

Ken had been distressed by the news as well, but he seemed to handle it better. Or at least more calmly than Molly. He'd sat on the porch, rocking in his favorite chair, as people came and went. Xander had sat beside him much of the time, trying to match his father's level temperament and failing.

Ken didn't have much to tell the police, of course, because he didn't know the truth. All he could tell them was that Tommy had run away and he could take a lie detector test to confirm it. Xander had been sitting with Ken at the kitchen table eating breakfast when Wade had come to them with the note left on Tommy's bed.

Xander had written the note himself, but he'd feigned surprise and chased after Ken when he'd rushed to the bunkhouse. There they'd found his bed hadn't been slept in and all of Tommy's things were gone. When asked, none of the boys said they had seen Tommy leave or knew where he could've gone. Ken had immediately called the police and turned over the letter. From there, the professionals had tried, and failed, to determine what had become of Tommy Wilder.

It was the same story Ken had always told. The same story Molly and Xander and everyone else told. It was all they knew to tell. The press and Sheriff Duke couldn't do much more than write down their statements and go home. There was no crime scene to study or evidence left to collect. Tommy's letter had been misplaced when the sheriff's department archived old case files years ago.

There was an old story and a body, and between them, a gap big enough for Tommy to disappear into it.

Heath had been worried that it wouldn't be enough, but it seemed to hold. Xander had planted enough seeds of doubt in the sheriff's mind that attention would eventually shift away from his family. Tommy had been a magnet for trouble, after all. That was a well-documented fact. It wasn't a stretch to suggest that perhaps Tommy had run off to meet someone. Maybe he'd been involved in dealing drugs or something else with dangerous and untrustworthy people. Anything could've happened to him once he left the safety of the bunkhouse.

All Xander needed was reasonable doubt and he was satisfied that he had it. Thankfully, he'd reached that point when he had. Congress would be back in session come Monday. He couldn't do anything more at the farm right now. The only other reason for him to stay in Cornwall was to work things out with Rose, and as much as he might want to do that, she was very firm about him staying away for a while.

So he went home. Once he was able to lose himself in his job again, maybe the sharp pain that stabbed him in the chest every time he thought of her would fade away.

Xander sipped the last of his Scotch and sighed. The liquor had done its work and numbed the darkest thoughts in his brain. Now perhaps he could get some sleep. He wasn't going to pass out on the stool at the kitchen island, so he needed to head upstairs. He left the glass on the counter and stumbled back to grab his bags. He hauled them up into his room and set them on the foot of the bed. His bigger bag could wait for the morning to be unpacked, but he needed his toiletries and things out of the smaller duffel that he used for his sleepovers at Rose's apartment.

Methodically, he went about unpacking it, setting aside his case of grooming items and a few other things. He was rummaging through some dirty clothes when his fingers brushed against something hard and rough in texture. He didn't recall packing anything like that, so he felt around until he found it again and pulled the item out to examine it.

Holding it in his hand, Xander glanced down and his mouth dropped open. He stumbled back to sit on the mattress before his knees gave out.

It was a picture frame. He remembered making one just like this when he went to scout camp twenty years ago. It was a craft project made of painted Popsicle sticks and backed with felt. Hard macaroni noodles were glued to the frame and decorated with puff paint and glitter.

The picture in the frame was of him, Rose and Joey under the Camp Middleton sign. He'd forgotten they'd even taken that picture until now. They looked just like a happy family in the photo. Joey was beaming with the excitement and anticipation of going to camp. Rose seemed nervous, but she hid it well from her son. Xander smiled awkwardly, as though he felt out of place, but Rose's grip on his arm kept him firmly in place. It was a nice picture of the three of them.

And then he looked at the words along the top. Spelled out in foam cutout letters was Dad, Mom & Me.

It was as though someone had punched him in the gut as hard as they could. Joey *knew.* They hadn't told him. Hadn't breathed a word of it, but he knew the truth. His son had made this picture frame for him at camp and slipped the gift into his bag when he wasn't looking. Probably while Xander was in the bedroom fighting with Rose.

His son gave him this gift and minutes later Xander had walked out of his son's life without a word of explanation. He felt sick. The Scotch that only a moment ago had soothed him was now churning in his belly and threatening to rise up into his throat.

What was he going to do? How could he convince Rose to let him back in their lives?

Xander had no intention of abandoning his son. It was bad enough that Joey had gone through the first ten years of his life without a father. But if the situation with Tommy took a turn for the worse, would it hurt his son more to have an absent father or, as Rose had pointed out, a criminal one?

He dropped his forehead into the palm of his hand and stared down at the picture. His son's eyes were so much like his own. He reminded him so much of himself when he was that age. The same age when he had lost his father.

It would be cruel to give Joey a father at last and then rip him away in the same breath.

Rose might not like it, but he wasn't going to stay away. He'd already kept his distance for far too long. No matter what happened on the farm this week or next week or next year, he would be a part of Joey's life. He wasn't going to walk away from his son.

Or the mother of his child.

Rose placed a curl of candied lemon peel as the finishing touch on her lemon chiffon cake. It was beautiful and delicious, the fifth dessert she'd made today. She slid it into the dessert display case and went back out front to check on a few of her diners at the counter.

It had been a month since the bake-off. Three weeks since she'd thrown Xander out of her apartment and tossed away their future together. In that short amount of time, things had changed very quickly for her.

First she was approached at the diner one afternoon by the man who owned three other eateries in the area. He was one of the judges of the bake-off and wanted to know if she was interested in providing all the desserts for his restaurants. One of his locations was a dinner-only establishment, so he offered her the kitchens to bake in the mornings. He even told her she could do any kind of baking she liked, even for other restaurants.

It wasn't enough to keep her from having to wait tables, but it was a start. The major impediment to starting her own baking business was getting the licenses and permits. She needed a dedicated kitchen that was subject to health inspections. That was something she simply couldn't afford, but using the restaurant kitchen was perfect. Making desserts for both places was a great supplement to her income and there was always the hope that it would lead to more work with other restaurants. Then maybe, one day, her own bakery.

It was the one bright thought she clung to during the darkest of days. Xander had been the one to suggest the idea of opening her own bakery and it had offered a welcome distraction. It gave her something to talk to Joey about where she didn't get upset. She didn't want to cry in front of her son. Then she might have to explain what was really going on and where Xander had gone.

She didn't know if he was still in town or not, but he had done as she asked and stayed away. It was probably easy for him with everything else happening. She wasn't entirely sure what was going on; she was avoiding the news as best she could. She already knew more about the situation than she'd ever wanted to.

Rose couldn't get away entirely, though. As she wiped down the counter, the sound of the local newscast taunted her from the other side of the counter. There was no way she could get away from it with the television in the diner always finding its way back to the local news every time she turned around.

"Rose, can you turn it up? They're talking about the body again."

"Which is why I turned it down, Paul. People are eating," Rose complained, but she still grabbed the remote off the counter and turned the volume up a few notches.

"Police have questioned the family that had owned the property for over thirty years, but they are not suspects at this time. Ken and Molly Eden reported Tommy missing the morning after he disappeared. What happened after Tommy left and how he ended up in that shallow grave is still a mystery."

"You must've known the dead kid," he pointed out. "You were going with one of the Eden boys back then, weren't you?"

"I was. And I did know him, but I didn't have much to do with him." She didn't elaborate. She wasn't keen to invite this topic of conversation. The news crews were hot for people to interview who might've known Tommy or the Edens back then. Rose didn't want any part of it.

Paul watched the television thoughtfully. "I've heard he was a pretty rotten sort. His own parents couldn't handle him, so the state took him away."

Rose nodded, pretending to listen, as she had every day since Tommy Wilder's body was identified. Instead she cleared a few empty plates, scooped a few dollars' tip into her apron pocket and went back into the kitchen to put the dirty dishes into the dish pile.

She hoped that by the time she returned, the segment would be over. And it was. It was fortunate since Paul was now gone and the flame-red hair of Tori Sullivan could be spotted at the far end of the counter. She was probably tired of the news, too.

"Hey, Rose," she said in greeting.

Rose put on her best smile and headed in that direction. She poured a glass of water and set it down in front of her. She wasn't unhappy to see Tori, but at the moment, she was trying to avoid anything to do with the Edens. Tori could be here to gossip, to get a piece of pie or to try and convince her not to be mad at Xander. She hoped it was the pie.

"What can I get you today? I just put out a beautiful lemon chiffon cake."

Her blue eyes lit up, and then disappointment crossed her delicate features. "I'd love to, but I can't."

"Why not?" If anyone deserved cake, it was people with police officers traipsing through their yard.

"The wedding is coming up. I had my dress fitting last week and the seamstress threatened my life if I gained or lost any weight. Mostly gained," she added with a smile. "That means no lemon chiffon cake for me."

Rose nodded sympathetically. "Well, if you find you've somehow lost weight without intending to, you march right down here and get some cake to get you back where you need to be."

Tori smiled widely. "I absolutely will."

So she wasn't here for dessert, Rose thought with a frown. "What about lunch, then?"

The woman eyed her, her pink lips twisting in thought. "I shouldn't. I really didn't come down here for food."

Shoot. Why couldn't it have been the pie?

"What can I do for you, then, Tori?" She wished she could say the restaurant was slammed and she didn't have time to chat, but they were the only two people in there at the moment. It was that odd time that was too late for lunch, too early for dinner. Things would pick up in an hour or so, but until then she had nothing better to do, apparently, than talk to Tori.

"I wanted to talk to you without the boys or anyone else around."

Rose leaned her elbows onto the counter. "About what?"

Tori tilted her head to the side like a confused puppy. "Come on, now, Rose. You can be honest with me. I mean, I know about Joey. This whole thing has to be hard on you."

The sympathetic words brought an unexpected rush of tears to her eyes. "It's okay. Really," she argued, snatching a napkin out of the nearby dispenser to halt the flow. "I never really envisioned a life with Xander in it."

"Liar," Tori said. "You know you've spent the last decade fantasizing about him being back in your life."

How did she know Rose so well? "And look what it got me, Tori. He's a criminal."

Tori nodded. "If Xander is a criminal, you know who else is? Wade. And I'm going to marry him anyway."

Rose was taken aback. She'd assumed that Tori knew about what had happened, and yet she hadn't ever considered that the wedding was happening despite that fact. "Did Wade tell you…?" Her voice trailed off.

"He told me some. The recent news has helped me piece together the rest of the story. But I believed it when Wade told me he'd do *anything* to protect his family and the people he loved, including me. Don't focus on what they might have done. Think about why. About how important it must have been to protect someone they cared about. You'd do anything for Joey, wouldn't you?"

Rose knew exactly how quickly her hackles got up where her son was concerned. Just thinking of when she got the call about him breaking his arm... If he was in true danger, she would do anything to protect him. "Of course."

"I don't know everything that happened that night, but I have to believe that it wasn't with malice aforethought." Tori smiled and shook her head. "Apparently, I've been watching too many crime shows trying to decompress from the wedding planning. But listen," she added, flicking the bright red waves of her hair over her shoulder. "I know that your father going to jail was hard on you. I can only imagine how difficult it made life here in Cornwall. Small towns are rough, and when it comes to not fitting in, I'm at the top of the list. I never fit in anywhere, not even here, before Wade.

"But you can't let other people's opinion of you—or someone in your family—dictate your life or your self-worth. You're not trash, Rose. Not your father or anyone else could make you that. You're a good person. A great mother. A fantastic pastry chef. That's way more important than the deeds of your family members."

Rose felt a rush of embarrassment reach her cheeks. "You don't need to say all those things, Tori."

"Yes, I do. Because you need to hear it. And you need to know that Xander and your father are two very different people committing two very different crimes. Xander would never deliberately hurt you like your father has. He loves you. And he loves Joey. He may not have said it, but I've seen that sad, moony look in his eyes. He misses you both so badly. I think it killed him to have to go back to D.C. with things unresolved between the two of you."

"He's gone?" Rose asked, and Tori nodded.

Rose shouldn't have been pleased to hear that Xander missed her, but somehow knowing he was suffering a little bit while they were apart was nice. He should at least be as miserable as she was, although she doubted he was. Tori might think Xander was in love with her, but he wasn't. He was in love with the idea of their family and being a dad. Now that he was home and surrounded by his old life, he'd forget all about that.

"I won't keep him away from Joey forever. I just need to make sure that whatever this is—" she gestured toward the television "—doesn't blow up. I don't want to tell my son who his father is only to have to visit him on Sunday afternoons during inmate visitation. I'd rather wait. We've waited this long."

"And what about you?"

"What?"

"You said you wouldn't keep Joey away from him forever. What about you? Are you going to keep your distance from the man you've loved since you were fifteen years old?"

"Maybe," Rose admitted.

"What could he do to convince you to give him another chance?"

Rose shook her head and turned to look out the window. The sheriff's car blew by, probably heading up to the Garden of Eden again. "I don't know that there's anything he can do, Tori. Maybe our chance ended back in the summer before college."

Tori's clear blue eyes were nearly penetrating as she looked at Rose. They were beautiful and icy, making her want to shiver in her uniform. After a moment, Tori got up from her chair and put a five-dollar bill on the counter even though she hadn't bothered to order.

"What's this for?" Rose said, holding up the bill.

"It's for working hard for far less money than you deserve. You're entitled to some happiness. You just have to be open to the possibilities. And it's possible that back in high school was just the beginning for you two," she said before slipping out of the diner and out of Rose's sight.

Thirteen

Things weren't exactly going as Xander had planned. He'd hoped to get back to Cornwall as soon as he could, but work got in the way and he found himself wrapped up in congressional committee sessions that lasted late into the night nearly every day.

It had taken him two weeks to get things in motion and he'd had to cash in a couple favors to get away, but he was two miles outside of Cornwall and closing in fast. But now that he was here, he had to wonder where everyone else was.

The town was quieter than usual for four o'clock in the afternoon. There weren't a lot of cars on the road. He drove out to Rose's apartment, but her car wasn't there. He cruised back to Daisy's, but her Honda wasn't there, either. No one was there, actually. He would have called Rose on her cell phone if he thought for a moment that she would answer.

Instead he headed to the town watering hole. There wasn't a single vehicle in the lot outside the Wet Hen, either, except for the bartender's old truck parked out back. Curious, Xander pulled in. The bartender, Skippy, would know where everyone was. He typically had the pulse of the town.

The skinny, leathery old man at the bar looked up when he came in. "Congressman Langston," he greeted with a casual wave. "What brings you to the Hen?"

It was a good question. Xander hadn't stepped foot in the place in years. Of course, it looked exactly the same as it had then. And the fifty years before then. And the fifty years before that. The Hen had opened in 1897 and aside from those newfangled electric lights and the cooling systems for the liquor and the patrons, not much had changed. He went to the bar and settled onto one of the worn leather stools.

"Afternoon, Skippy. I came into town for the weekend and I can't seem to find anyone around. Any idea where they've all gone?"

Skippy nodded and leaned up against the bar where Xander had seated himself. "Everyone's probably at the ball field. The local Little League team made it to the final four in the state championships. Tonight they're playing their last game. If they win it, they'll play the other winner for the state title. People have really gotten excited about it. It's all they've talked about on the news lately.

"I'm kinda relieved," Skippy added. "I'm tired of all that nonsense about your folks' place. That Wilder kid could've found trouble wherever you put him. Did you know I actually caught him stealing liquor out of the back room once? Who knows what he got himself into? Harassing good people like the Edens won't get Sheriff Duke anywhere."

Xander was glad to at least have Skippy on their side. He probably had more pull in town than the mayor did. People were very suggestible when drunk. "Thanks, Skippy. Do you know what time the game was supposed to start?"

Skippy eyed his watch. "About a half hour ago. You'd better hurry on if you're going to see your boy play. He got his cast off a few days ago. Doc cleared him to play with a brace as long as he wears his glove and catches with his right hand."

Xander's gaze met Skippy's weary dark eyes and the old man smiled. Skippy truly knew everything that went on in this town. It was a little scary. Thankfully, time had proven that Skippy kept most of his knowledge to himself. "Uh…thanks again. I'll see you around." He slid off the stool and bolted from the bar.

The community ball field was about five miles away. It wouldn't take him long to get there. It did, however, take him a while to park. Everyone, and it really was everyone, had come out to support the team.

He found a spot in a lot about a block away. Little League games were only six innings, so he worried he might have missed it entirely, but everyone was still at the field and he could see the little boys in the outfield as he got closer. Xander glanced at the scoreboard. It was the bottom of the fifth inning. Joey's team, the Litchfield Lions, was ahead by two runs. A glance at the crowd gathered around the field was intimidating. They'd spilled off the bleachers and lined the sides in lawn chairs and blankets. He tried to spy Rose in the stands, but there were so many people.

The crowd shouted encouraging words to the boys as the Lions struck out and the team ran to take their positions in the outfield. Xander took the opportunity to get people's attention without distracting the players. "Rose!" he shouted. "Rose Pierce!"

Quite a few people turned in his direction, but she was

not one of them. "She's at the top of the bleachers by the Lions' dugout," someone yelled.

"Thanks!" Xander stepped through the crowd, dodging folks with popcorn and soda. With the area narrowed down, he was finally able to spot Rose sitting beside her brother, Craig. She was wearing a bright blue Litchfield Lions T-shirt and her hair was pulled back into a ponytail. She didn't see him. She was fully focused on the game.

Xander stopped at the bottom of the bleachers. This was it. The moment. His heart raced like election night, but he wouldn't let his nerves get the better of him. He performed best under pressure, right?

Rose's gaze met his then, and she froze. A flash of surprise, then fear, then concern crossed her face before it went blank. Xander started climbing up the bleachers, cutting through the cluster of people and nearly stepping on a couple to reach the top.

This probably wasn't the best conversation to have in public. With the whole town watching. He'd prefer to have this moment in a dark, romantic restaurant or, at the very least, without his scowling future brother-in-law there to witness the whole thing. But that was the hand fate had dealt him. At the very least, she couldn't cause a scene. Rose didn't like attention being drawn to her. She would have to sit there and listen to what he had to say.

Xander stopped on the metal bench directly ahead of her. He squatted down, carefully balancing where she couldn't avoid looking at him.

"What do you want, Xander?" Her voice was cold and angry, but he wouldn't be deterred by that.

"I want to talk to you."

"We've talked enough. I've told you to leave us alone. Now get out of the way so I can watch my son play."

Craig suddenly stood up. "I need a drink." He gestured

for Xander to take his seat as he stepped out toward the concession stand.

"Thanks," Xander said, plopping down beside her.

"Craig!" Rose complained, but it was too late. She sighed and inched away from him, although there wasn't really anyplace she could go.

Xander sat awkwardly beside her for a moment before he said anything else. "How is Joey playing? Is his arm holding up okay?"

Her eyes were focused on the field as she spoke. "He's doing well. The arm doesn't seem to be holding him back. He made a run in the third inning."

"I'm glad he got his cast off in time to play."

"Me too," she said, seeming to grow more comfortable as they focused on the safe territory of their son.

"I love you, Rose."

That finally drew her attention, as well as the attention of several people sitting around them. Rose's pale skin took on a pinkish hue of embarrassment. "Xander, shhh!" she said with wide eyes.

"Shhh?" Xander repeated. "That's not exactly what I was hoping to hear."

Her lips twisted with anxiety. "Well, both of us seem to be suffering from disappointment lately." She turned back to the game and cheered enthusiastically at the boys on the field.

"No one is perfect, Rose. Not me, not you. Perhaps we've both built up this fantasy of one another since our high school days. I'm sorry I haven't lived up to your expectations. But you've got to believe me when I say the only crime I'm guilty of is loving you too much."

Rose didn't respond, but she'd stopped cheering and seemed to be listening intently despite refusing to look at him.

"We've all made mistakes. We've all got secrets. Believe me when I say that if I could go back, there are a couple of things I would do differently. The first would be letting you walk away from me all those years ago. It's my biggest regret. But I'm not going to make the same mistake twice. I'm not going to let you push me away again."

Xander reached out to caress her cheek and gently turn her to face him. "I know you're scared, Rose. So am I. But these last few weeks I've realized that the reality of losing you is far worse than the fear of what might happen if I came back here and told you how I felt.

"I want to focus on my future. *Our* future. You and me and Joey together the way a family should be. I don't want anything you and I did in the past to come in the way of that." Xander reached into his pocket and grasped the small velvet box in his fist.

"Xander," Rose began, but stopped when she saw the box.

"I had this made for you. There's only one other ring like it in the whole world." He held it out and opened the lid on the hinge. "My hope is that you will wear this one every day of the rest of your life."

It couldn't be. It just couldn't be.

It was surreal enough to have Xander here, telling Rose that he loved her. Tori had told her as much was true, although she hadn't believed her. Having him produce an engagement ring was beyond her most secret of fantasies. But then he opened the box and the world tilted sideways.

Her mother's engagement ring. At least, it looked like her engagement ring. After the cancer claimed her, Rose's mother had been buried with her wedding ring and engagement ring on her finger. Xander had had it re-created for her.

With her hand shaking, Rose reached out for the ring and then gripped the platinum band tightly to keep from dropping it under the bleachers. Upon closer inspection, she could tell it wasn't a perfect replica. For one thing, her mother's ring had been white gold, not platinum. And the sideways oval diamond inset into the band was much larger and sparkled brighter than any stone her father could ever afford.

But the band had the same intricate crisscrossed mount with cutaways that revealed more tiny diamonds, just as her mother's ring had. "How did you ever find a ring like my mother's?"

"Like I said, I had it made. With help from Craig, if you can believe it."

Rose tore her gaze away from the sparkling ring to frown at Xander in disbelief. "Craig helped you?"

"He did." Xander smiled. "He sent me pictures of the ring so I could have a jeweler in D.C. re-create it for you. Do you like it?"

Rose's mouth dropped open to answer, but she couldn't find the words. Of course she loved it. It was absolutely perfect. Beautiful, sentimental and thoughtful, as Xander always tried to be. The issue was whether or not she could accept it.

"Okay, now I have to ask you an important question. Two, actually. First," he said, taking the ring from her fingers, "will you, Rosalyn Pierce, give me the honor of your hand in marriage?"

She had been beating herself up for weeks thinking about her last conversation with Xander. How she'd reacted but not listened. How she'd painted him with her father's brush without giving him the chance to explain how they were different. Tori had been right. She would do anything for Joey. And she knew that Xander would do anything for his family, and that included her and their son. Her father had never cared about anyone but himself.

Saying yes was a risk. Things were still unresolved with the police. But she was more frightened by the idea of saying no and losing him again. She loved him. He accepted her past and the flaws in it. If she wanted to be happy, she needed to do the same.

"Yes," Rose replied. The answer was barely audible with the cheering in the stands around them, but Xander pushed the ring onto her finger and smiled, so he'd heard her.

"The second question," he said, "is will you come live with me in D.C.? That town house is so lonely since you left."

She nodded, although the movement was barely visible before he scooped her into his arms and captured her mouth in a kiss. She melted against him, the heat of the late-summer ball game nowhere near as scorching as the desire building up inside of her.

"I love you, Rose," he whispered against her lips.

Rose pulled away to look into his eyes. "I love you, too, Xander."

A cheer went up and the crowd around them leaped to their feet. They both stood to try and figure out what they'd missed. It didn't take long. It was the top of the sixth, two strikes, and the Lions were still ahead. If the other team didn't score, the game was over and Joey's team went to the championship.

Xander reached out for her hand with his own and his fingers entwined with hers. They both waited, barely breathing as the next boy came up to bat. He swung hard at the pitch and it was a pop fly heading straight for Joey in his position as shortstop.

"Oh no," Rose said, covering her mouth with her other

hand. "I hope he can catch that with the glove on the wrong hand."

It seemed like forever for the ball to come down and when it did, it was nestled safely in Joey's glove. The game was over. The roar from the surrounding spectators was near deafening. Parents anxiously waited for the teams to give high fives to one another and practice good sportsmanship and then poured onto the grass to celebrate with their kids.

Xander helped Rose down the steps and they found Joey still standing between second and third base, holding the winning ball. He seemed a little stunned.

"Congratulations, baby." Rose let go of Xander's hand to swoop in and gather her son in her arms. "You played an excellent game tonight. Best catch ever."

"Thanks," Joey said with a grin, and then his eyes widened as they looked over her shoulder. "Xander?"

Her son pulled away to rush Xander as he crouched in the dirt near third base. He caught the boy in his arms, still cautious of the sturdy black brace on his left arm. "Good job, kiddo."

"I'm glad you made it, Dad."

"I'm glad I made it, too."

"Wait, what?" Rose said. They hadn't had that discussion with him yet. Xander didn't even flinch. He just smiled wide, his hazel eyes getting a touch glassy.

Xander patted Joey on the shoulder and stood, turning back to her. "He already knew, Rose. He's more observant than we gave him credit for."

"How did you know?"

"Joey left a gift for me in my luggage."

"Did you like it?" Joey perked up.

Xander grinned. "It was the best macaroni-and-

Popsicle-stick picture frame ever made in the history of camp."

"I think we need to go get some ice cream to celebrate," Rose said.

"Celebrate my win?" Joey asked.

"And some other things." Rose wiggled her fingers and Joey's eyes went to the diamond on her hand.

"You guys are getting married? That's awesome! Are we moving to D.C.? Will I get to meet the president?"

"Whoa, kiddo," Xander said with a smile. "One thing at a time. Let's start with ice cream."

"Xander James Langston!" A woman's sharp voice cut through the crowd.

"Uh-oh."

Rose, Xander and Joey all turned and found a red-faced Molly Eden standing a few feet away in a Litchfield Lions T-shirt and jeans. She was usually the spitting image of sweetness and Christmas spirit—a few years and a few pounds from being a walking, talking Mrs. Claus. She looked anything but sweet at the moment. She looked as if she'd caught them sneaking back in after curfew and was about to wear Xander's rear end out.

Her hands were planted on her hips, her furious gaze shifting between Rose and Xander. Then it was interrupted by a smile curling her lips when she looked at Joey. Ken was behind her, a gentle, restraining hand on her shoulder and a smug grin on his face. Thank goodness for Ken.

"Mama…" Xander started, but he was silenced by Molly raising her hand.

"Don't start." She pointed to Joey. "Is *that* my grandson?"

Rose watched Xander swallow hard and take a deep breath. He looked as though he'd sooner take on Sheriff Duke. "Yes."

"My *ten-year-old* grandson?" she clarified.

Rose felt the need to intervene on his behalf. "Yes, but he didn't know until a few weeks ago."

Molly nodded. She seemed to accept the excuse, but Rose got the feeling that neither of them were off the hook. "It's a wonder you kept it a secret that long, Rosalyn. He looks just like Xander did when he came to live with us."

"I'm sorry, Mrs. Eden."

"Lord," Molly said, eyeing the ring on Rose's hand and throwing her hands up. "I think you'd better start calling me Mama. Or maybe Grandma. I thought I'd have more time to get used to the name, but here we are."

Molly turned to focus on their son and a warm smile spread across her face. She took a few steps toward Joey and bent over to look at him eye level. It wouldn't be long before he was taller than her. "I've been waiting a long time for a grandchild. Do you like cookies?"

"I've been waiting a long time for grandparents. And I love cookies."

Tears rushed to Molly's eyes and Rose felt a similar prickle. "Oh!" Molly gushed, reaching forward to pull the little boy into her arms. "I'm a grandmother!" she yelled to the crowd. A few people turned to look at them with surprise on their faces, but most were still wrapped up in the team's celebration.

"That went better than I expected," Xander whispered as he leaned into Rose.

Rose rested her head against his chest and sighed. Everything had gone better than she'd expected. She just had to let go of her fear. Well, maybe not all of it.

Molly's sharp green gaze turned to Xander and her smile flattened to a frown of displeasure. "You two," she added, "will be dealt with after I get done enjoying my grandbaby."

Epilogue

Molly and Ken sat in chairs on the back porch watching Xander and their grandson ride around on a four-wheeler. Rose was on the stairs, watching nervously. Joey was wearing a helmet, but that hardly made her feel better. She'd just gotten her son out of the brace. She wasn't eager to get a new one put on him. They had a busy few weeks ahead of them. They were finished packing and would leave tomorrow to move down to Washington. They had to get Joey enrolled in school and get settled in a new place. Another injury would certainly handicap the process.

Her attention was pulled away by the sound of a car coming up the gravel drive. It was Sheriff Duke's squad car. Her heart sank in her chest. She didn't know what this was about, but a personal visit from the sheriff was never good. The previous sheriff had been the one to come and tell her what her father had done. He'd also told Xander his parents were dead.

The sheriff climbed from his car and made his way over to the back porch. Rose leaped up from her spot and took her place to the right of Molly's chair.

"Molly, Ken, Rosalyn," Sheriff Duke said, acknowledging them and frowning as he came up the stairs. "I hate to do this, Ken, but I'm going to have to bring you in for questioning."

"What?" Molly said, leaping up from her chair. "Questioning about what, Sheriff Duke?"

Rose immediately put her arms around Molly's shoulders. "Xander!" she cried out into the yard, but he was already on his way.

He climbed up the back steps two at a time with Joey in his wake. "What's all this about?" he asked.

The sheriff shuffled uncomfortably in his shoes. "I need to take Ken to the station for some official questioning."

She watched as Xander's jaw stiffened and his blank politician's expression fell over his features. "Has there been a break in the case? Last I heard, you didn't have any leads on what happened after Tommy ran away."

"You know full well I can't tell you details about the case, Congressman. The trail leaves off here at the farm and that's where I intend to pick it up. Let's please not make a scene about this."

"Are you arresting him?" Molly asked, her green eyes wide in horror.

"Did he say that, Molly?" Ken said, easing up stiffly from his chair. "He just said he had questions. I'd have questions if I were in his shoes, but there's nothing to worry about."

"I don't like this, Dad," Xander said. "You've already answered all their questions. What's really going on, Sheriff?"

Sheriff Duke tightened his jaw and sighed. "Someone

killed a kid on your property, Ken. People want to see some progress on this case."

"So you're hauling in an innocent man to make your department look more effectual?" Rose couldn't keep the words from flying from her lips, unhelpful as they might be.

"We're narrowing down our suspect list," Sheriff Duke said, his brow furrowing in irritation.

"Oh, Lord," Molly wailed. "You can't possibly think Ken killed Tommy."

"Someone did, Molly." Sheriff Duke took off his hat and ran his hand over the bald dome of his head in exasperation. "Should I bring Julianne in for questioning instead? Maybe Heath? They were only thirteen when Tommy disappeared, but you never know with kids anymore."

"This is ridiculous," Xander said, cutting off his mother before she gave the sheriff a piece of her mind for daring to insinuate her babies were involved. "Dad, that's it. I don't want you going in. Not without an attorney present. We'll call Frank Hartman first. If the sheriff wants you to answer questions, let him arrest you. Otherwise," Xander said, turning to face the barrel-chested man, "we're done here."

Sheriff Duke sighed and reached to his belt for his handcuffs. "Fine. Ken Eden, you're under arrest for the murder of Thomas Wilder. Anything you say can and will be u—"

"Grandpa!" Joey yelled in alarm.

Everyone turned to look at Ken, whose face had drained of blood and looked an ashy white. His breathing was labored, his hand reaching out to steady himself on Xander's shoulder.

"Ken? Are you okay?" Sheriff Duke asked.

"I can't…" he gasped. "My h-heart…" he managed to say before losing consciousness and slipping to the porch with a dull thud.

* * * * *

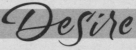

REQUEST YOUR FREE BOOKS!
2 FREE NOVELS PLUS 2 FREE GIFTS!

♦ HARLEQUIN®

Desire

ALWAYS POWERFUL, PASSIONATE AND PROVOCATIVE

YES! Please send me 2 FREE Harlequin Desire® novels and my 2 FREE gifts (gifts are worth about $10). After receiving them, if I don't wish to receive any more books, I can return the shipping statement marked "cancel." If I don't cancel, I will receive 6 brand-new novels every month and be billed just $4.55 per book in the U.S. or $4.99 per book in Canada. That's a savings of at least 13% off the cover price! It's quite a bargain! Shipping and handling is just 50¢ per book in the U.S. and 75¢ per book in Canada.* I understand that accepting the 2 free books and gifts places me under no obligation to buy anything. I can always return a shipment and cancel at any time. Even if I never buy another book, the two free books and gifts are mine to keep forever.

225/326 HDN F4ZC

Name	(PLEASE PRINT)
Address	Apt. #
City	State/Prov.	Zip/Postal Code
Signature (if under 18, a parent or guardian must sign)	

Mail to the **Harlequin® Reader Service:**

IN U.S.A.: P.O. Box 1867, Buffalo, NY 14240-1867
IN CANADA: P.O. Box 609, Fort Erie, Ontario L2A 5X3

**Want to try two free books from another line?
Call 1-800-873-8635 or visit www.ReaderService.com.**

* Terms and prices subject to change without notice. Prices do not include applicable taxes. Sales tax applicable in N.Y. Canadian residents will be charged applicable taxes. Offer not valid in Quebec. This offer is limited to one order per household. Not valid for current subscribers to Harlequin Desire books. All orders subject to credit approval. Credit or debit balances in a customer's account(s) may be offset by any other outstanding balance owed by or to the customer. Please allow 4 to 6 weeks for delivery. Offer available while quantities last.

Your Privacy—The Harlequin® Reader Service is committed to protecting your privacy. Our Privacy Policy is available online at www.ReaderService.com or upon request from the Harlequin Reader Service.

We make a portion of our mailing list available to reputable third parties that offer products we believe may interest you. If you prefer that we not exchange your name with third parties, or if you wish to clarify or modify your communication preferences, please visit us at www.ReaderService.com/consumerschoice or write to us at Harlequin Reader Service Preference Service, P.O. Box 9062, Buffalo, NY 14269. Include your complete name and address.

HD13R

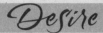
Beth stood and went to the ladder, peering up at their prison door. "I don't hear anything at all," she said. "What if we have to spend the night here? I don't want to sleep on the concrete floor. And I'm hungry, dammit."

Drew heard the moment she cracked. Jumping to his feet, he took her in his arms and shushed her. He let her cry it out, surmising that the tears were healthy. This afternoon had been scary as hell, and to make things worse, they had no clue if help was on the way and no means of communication.

Beth felt good in his arms. Though he usually had the urge to argue with her, this was better. Her hair was silky, the natural curls alive and bouncing with vitality. Though he had felt the pull of sexual attraction between them before, he had never acted on it. Now, trapped in the dark with nothing to do, he wondered what would happen if he kissed her.

Wondering led to fantasizing, which led to action.

Tangling his fingers in the hair at her nape, he tugged back her head and looked at her, wishing he could see her expression. "Better now?" The crying was over except for the occasional hitching breath.

"Yes." He felt her nod.

"I want to kiss you, Beth. But you can say no."

She lifted her shoulders and let them fall. "You saved my life. I suppose a kiss is in order."

He frowned. "We saved *each other's* lives," he said firmly. "I'm not interested in kisses as legal tender."

"Oh, just do it," she said, the words sharp instead of romantic. "We've both thought about this over the last two years. Don't deny it."

He brushed the pad of his thumb over her lower lip. "I wasn't planning to."

When their lips touched, something spectacular happened. Time stood still. Not as it had in the frantic fury of the storm, but with a hushed anticipation.

Don't miss the first installment of the

**TEXAS CATTLEMAN'S CLUB:
AFTER THE STORM** *miniseries,*

STRANDED WITH THE RANCHER

by USA TODAY *bestselling author*

Janice Maynard.

Available October 2014 wherever Harlequin® Desire books and ebooks are sold.

POWERFUL HEROES... SCANDALOUS SECRETS... BURNING DESIRES!

TEMPTED BY A COWBOY
by Sarah M. Anderson

Available October 2014

The 2nd novel of the *Beaumont Heirs* featuring one Colorado family with limitless scandal!

How can she resist the cowboy's smile when it promises so much pleasure?

Phillip Beaumont likes his drinks strong and his women easy. So why is he flirting with his new horse trainer, Jo Spears, who challenges him at every turn? Phillip wants nothing but the chase...until the look in Jo's haunted green eyes makes him yearn for more....

Sure, Jo's boss is as jaded and stubborn as Sun, the multimillion-dollar stallion she was hired to train. But it isn't long before she starts spending days *and* nights with the sexy cowboy. Maybe Sun isn't the only male on the Beaumont ranch worth saving!

Be sure to read the 1st novel of the *Beaumont Heirs*
by Sarah M. Anderson
NOT THE BOSS'S BABY

Available wherever books and ebooks are sold.

HD73346